7th Heaven™

SECRETS

by Amanda Christie

Based on the hit TV series
created by Brenda Hampton

And based on the following episodes:
"Sin..."
Written by Catherine LePard

"...And Expiation"
Written by Catherine LePard

Random House 🏠 New York

7th Heaven ™ & © 2000 Spelling Television Inc.
All rights reserved. Produced under license by
Random House, Inc.

All rights reserved under International and
Pan-American Copyright Conventions. Published
in the United States by Random House, Inc.,
New York, and simultaneously in Canada by
Random House of Canada Limited, Toronto.

www.randomhouse.com/kids

Library of Congress Catalog Card Number: 00-132046
ISBN: 0-553-49359-0

Printed in the United States of America
June 2000
10 9 8 7 6 5 4 3 2 1

RANDOM HOUSE and colophon are registered trademarks
of Random House, Inc.

ONE

Mary pushed her way through the locker room door and strode into the hallway outside the gym. She was surprised to find the gym doors still shut and her teammates milling around.

Some girls were already warming up, dribbling around other girls who were gossiping, stretching, or rechecking their sneakers.

Karen, a first-string senior like Mary, flipped her long ponytail over her shoulder and said, "Coach Cleary is late, and I need to practice my fast break."

"Yeah, you sure do," Mary replied. "Your fast break wasn't fast enough last Friday."

"Button it up, Camden!" Karen shot

back. "We *won*, didn't we?"

"Just barely," Elaine, another senior, added.

Karen darted around Mary and deftly snatched a ball from one of the freshman second-stringers. She bounced the ball, then shot it to Corey, another first-string player.

"Go Wildcats!" someone cried as Corey and Karen vied for the basketball. Mary clapped her hands as Karen rushed for an imaginary basket over the gym's double doors.

Corey ducked under Karen's arms and slipped past. As Karen spun, Corey jumped and sank the ball in the invisible hoop.

"Another score for the Wildcats!" Corey cried, throwing up her hands.

Karen smiled as she retrieved the ball. "Just two more games like Friday's and we'll beat the all-school record."

"The Lady Wildcats are the very best girls' varsity team in Glenoak history," Corey said proudly. "And it's all because of us."

"We're number one!" Karen whooped.

"And we're well on our way to the regional championship," Mary added with pride.

"How about two out of three?" Karen asked as she crouched low, holding the ball firmly in her grip.

Corey lunged, but Karen was faster. She slipped by Corey and rushed the imaginary basket.

Suddenly there was a loud clang as the heavy fire door down the hall slammed shut. All eyes turned.

Coach Cleary was coming.

Karen skidded to a halt and thrust the basketball behind her back. Everyone on the team knew that Coach Cleary frowned on horseplay in the hallway.

When the coach reached the girls, he paused, setting a gym bag on the floor in front of them.

The exuberance of a few moments before vanished when they saw Coach Cleary's icy expression. Only the senior first-stringers failed to notice the coach's mood. They refused to settle down even after he cleared his throat to get their attention.

"Anybody want to take a guess as to what I'm holding here?" Coach Cleary asked loudly, drowning out the chatter. He held up a thick file folder he'd pulled from the gym bag.

"A break that'll help us against Beecher's full-court press?" Corey replied, still smiling.

"We could use it," someone cried.

"I wish," Coach Cleary said tautly.

"Is that Beecher's scouting report on us?" Mary chimed in, trying to lighten the mood.

The faint hint of a smile tugged at Coach Cleary's lips. "I'd love to take a look at that, too, but no," he replied.

His eyes scanned the faces arrayed before him. "Anyone else care to guess?"

"The names and addresses of all the women who won't go out with you?" Karen added. Her words were greeted with a ripple of nervous laughter.

"That's a much, much thicker file," Coach Cleary said, shaking his head. "No, ladies," he continued, his tone serious. "These files are the academic progress reports I've been asking your teachers for every week since the basketball season started."

Some of the girls shifted uncomfortably and sneakers squeaked on the linoleum floor.

"These files sure make for some interesting reading," the coach continued. "I've read these files, and the ones that came before them, over and over again. And do you know what?"

No girl spoke.

"These files always say the same thing."

The hallway was so quiet that you could hear a pin drop. Mary Camden leaned against the wall and gazed at her feet. She, like many of her teammates, didn't like where this conversation was headed.

Coach Cleary opened the gym bag and dropped the folder inside. When he spoke again, his words were filled with disappointment.

"These files say that, in spite of the many warnings I've given all of you over the past few weeks, your grades have continued their downward spiral."

He paused for effect. "Except, of course, for the hardworking few who've maintained their fragile grip on academic mediocrity."

Coach Cleary's eyes were filled with resolve—and a deep sadness.

"I understand that some of this weak academic showing is due to 'senioritis,'" he continued. "But, frankly, I don't care."

Hands on his hips, Coach Cleary studied their faces.

"You were told in no uncertain terms that your studies were the priority, and your grades had to show immediate improvement. Unfortunately, these progress reports show that they haven't.

"I don't know if you didn't have an understanding of how serious I was or if you didn't have enough time to study, but..."

He reached down into his bag and pulled out a bicycle chain. He turned his back on the girls and looped it around the gym's door handles. Then he locked the chain in place with a padlock.

The coach turned and faced the girls again.

"Now you have both time and an understanding of just how serious I was."

"Practice is canceled?" Elaine cried in disbelief.

Coach Cleary lifted his gym bag and faced Elaine. The senior took a step backward when she saw the expression on his face.

"You are *students* who play basketball,"

Coach Cleary said. *"Not* basketball players who drop by classes when the mood strikes you. Until you show me that you understand what I'm saying—by bringing your grades up—this team and this season are *canceled."*

Mary heard a sharp intake of breath. She realized it was her own.

Before she or any of her teammates could protest, Coach Cleary walked down the hall and disappeared around the corner without another word.

In another part of Glenoak's Kennedy High School, Mary's younger sister Lucy was watching Principal Russell bang a wooden gavel.

"Student court is now in session!" Ms. Russell announced.

Lucy sat at a long table with the other student members of the court. She was filled with a mixture of pride and worry at carrying out this major new responsibility.

Look at them all, she thought, staring at the room full of fellow students. *They're all here to face our judgment.*

Just remember what Mom and Dad taught you about being fair and weighing decisions, she told herself, trying to calm down and pay attention. *And don't say anything stupid.*

When the room was quiet, Principal Russell studied the notes on her clipboard.

"Okay," she announced. "First up is Mr. Donnelly, Theresa Harvey, and Kevin Dorce. Step forward, please."

Mr. Donnelly, a teacher, rose and led two students to the front of the courtroom.

Ms. Russell was about to speak when Kevin Dorce took Theresa Harvey's hand in his. Their eyes met, and before anyone could say another word they began to make out, right in front of everyone in the courtroom!

Nervous giggles filled the room.

As Principal Russell watched with growing embarrassment, Mr. Donnelly gestured at the couple.

"See my problem?" the teacher asked.

"So...this...this happens often?" Lucy Camden stammered, averting her eyes.

"All the time!" Mr. Donnelly replied.

Then the teacher thrust a file folder between the couple. They broke their embrace and blinked at the court as if they'd just woken up.

Ms. Russell sighed and rubbed her

head. "Anything to say, you two?"

The couple shrugged.

"The court will announce its decision on Wednesday," said the principal. "Next case!"

A member of the freshman class approached the bench and laid his hand-written paper before the court. His teacher set down a reference book with the pages marked.

Lucy studied the report, then the pages in the book. Her eyes went wide.

"This is plagiarism," she cried. "You didn't even put this into your own words! You might as well have just photocopied the pages."

The freshman slapped his forehead. "I should have thought of that!" he muttered.

Principal Russell pressed her fingers to her temples again and rolled her eyes. Then she slammed the gavel down.

"Decision on Wednesday," she declared.

"Next up is David Dawes," Lucy Camden announced.

David held a wad of notes in his hand. Lucy leafed through them and looked up.

"You've had fifty-two podiatrist appointments?" she asked incredulously.

David Dawes shrugged. Ms. Russell

scanned the notes after Lucy.

"I compliment your spelling," the principal said after a moment. "You've spelled a difficult word like 'podiatrist' correctly."

David Dawes smiled proudly.

"Unfortunately," the principal added, "your mother spells her name with a K. On these notes, you spell Catherine with a C."

"No way!" David Dawes cried.

"*Way*, Mr. Dawes," Ms. Russell shot back. "There is more than one way to spell Catherine."

David Dawes shrugged. "Who knew?"

The boy jumped when the gavel banged again.

"Decision on Wednesday."

T W O

Across town, Matt Camden entered his apartment after a long day of college classes. It was after three in the afternoon, and he hadn't eaten since breakfast.

Matt sighed to himself when he saw his roommate, John Hamilton, sitting at the dining room table. Once again, the guy had covered every flat surface in sight with all his notebooks and textbooks.

"Hey, guys!" said John, looking up.

"Hey," said Matt's girlfriend Shana with a wave as she followed Matt through the door. The couple dumped their books on a chair and shed their jackets.

"You must have gotten back late last night," Matt said. "I didn't even hear you come in."

John sighed. "I was studying until the library closed. Then I moved to the coffee shop until they closed, and then I moved to the Student Union's all-night study lounge."

"Must be a big test," Matt said as he headed for the tiny kitchen with Shana.

John glanced at his wristwatch. "The test is coming up in half an hour. Unfortunately, I'm more than half an hour not ready."

"I've been there myself," Matt said with a nod.

He opened the refrigerator and peered inside. Matt frowned as he studied the emptiness within. "Been here before, too," he sighed.

"What are you guys up to?" John asked.

"We've got an hour until chem lab and we're starving to death," Matt said, still staring into the empty refrigerator.

Shana peered over Matt's shoulder. "All you have is baking soda and a battery?"

Matt closed the refrigerator, wishing— not for the first time—that he was back home. The Camden household might be a chaotic frenzy of fighting kids and bawling babies, but the fridge was always well stocked.

Shana began tearing through the kitchen, opening cupboards and peeking into empty cereal boxes, trying to find something to eat.

When the search came up empty, Matt shot his roommate an accusing stare.

"Don't look at me," John said with a shrug. "I haven't eaten anything today."

"Well, somebody needs to hit the store."

"Right," John said, sounding annoyed. "I'll leave a note for the maid."

Matt spied a pack of chewing gum half-buried under John's notebook. "Are you going to finish that?"

John shrugged as he tossed the chewing gum to Matt, who offered a stick to Shana. They chewed quietly for a minute.

"Well, it *almost* feels like eating," Shana said wistfully.

Back at the Camden household, Reverend Camden studied the twins with growing disbelief. He didn't think it was possible to actually *drip* with peanut butter, but little Samuel and David had managed it.

How could a simple snack have gone so terribly wrong? he asked himself.

Reverend Camden grabbed David and

placed the sticky baby in the kitchen sink.
Then he put Sam next to his brother.

Reverend Camden grabbed the dishwashing sprayer and briefly considered
using it. But he knew his wife would be
home any minute, and that she would not
approve.

He filled the sink and carefully began
washing the babies, who splashed around
as if it were a game. Within a few minutes,
Reverend Camden was more wet than the
babies.

He heard a door slam in the foyer—
generally a sign of trouble.

Reverend Camden moved to investi-
gate, then realized he had a sink full of
twins to deal with before he could go anywhere. So he strained his ears, trying to listen as angry voices filled the next room...

"It's not like I hurt anyone!" Simon
protested, his arms crossed.

"I don't care about that," Mrs. Camden
insisted. "What you did was wrong."

"But I didn't mean anything by it!"
Simon continued.

"Then why did you do it?" Mrs.
Camden shot back, hustling Ruthie
through the door.

"It's just a gesture. Nobody was hurt," Simon insisted. "And other than my friend, *you're* the only one who saw me do it."

"Me and *your principal*, Ms. Gordon."

Ruthie looked at Simon, then up at her mother.

"What's that finger thing mean, anyway?" she asked innocently.

Mrs. Camden looked hard at Simon.

"See what you've done?" she said.

Simon hung up his coat, still shaking his head.

"What you did was an incredibly rude, vulgar gesture that should never be done in public, or anywhere else for that matter," said Mrs. Camden, her patience wearing thin. "You're lucky you still have those fingers, mister."

"But Mom!" Simon cried. "My friends and I always do that kind of stuff. It's a guy thing."

Mrs. Camden stamped her foot. "It is *not* a guy thing."

Simon ran up the steps. Halfway up, he turned and faced his mother. "What do you know about being a guy, anyway?"

Mrs. Camden opened her mouth to speak, but realized she had no answer.

Reverend Camden entered the foyer,

carrying the twins in a laundry basket. Mrs. Camden blinked when she saw the babies.

"Peanut butter disaster," Reverend Camden explained. "I was washing them off when I heard the door slam. Is everything okay?"

Mrs. Camden sighed.

"When I pulled up in front of the school, *your* son was making a gesture with not *one*, but both hands—*fingers*, actually."

Reverend Camden paled. "Fingers?"

"And let me just say that *your* son wasn't hitchhiking, hailing a cab, or saying 'come hither.' He was making a very rude gesture!"

Reverend Camden's mouth opened in surprise.

"On top of that," she continued, "Principal Gordon also saw *your* son not making a peace sign, and the three of us have an appointment to see her tomorrow, in her office."

"Yikes," Reverend Camden said.

Mrs. Camden pushed past him, heading for the kitchen.

"What kind of mess will I find in *my* kitchen?" she cried over her shoulder.

"Oh, honey," Reverend Camden said, following her. "About the mess..."

At the top of the stairs, Simon sat with his head buried in his hands.

He had overheard every word his mother had spoken to his father, and they had hurt.

Why is it so hard to be a guy in this house? Simon wondered. *I can't let go for a minute. I always have to be the good son, the good example to Ruthie.*

He shook his head.

Why does everybody have to make such a big deal about a couple of fingers?

As he headed for his room, Simon felt the house close in on him, until it seemed as if he couldn't breathe.

Matt's lucky, Simon decided as he hopped onto his bed and curled up next to his dog, Happy. *He's old enough to move out. He doesn't have to listen to everything Mom says, or be a good example to his sisters.*

I can't wait until I'm free like Matt...

"What a mess!" Matt cried out to his empty apartment.

He had just gotten back from chem lab and it was already time to change into his hospital uniform and head for work.

Now Matt stood over a pile of laundry that threatened to engulf an entire corner of his tiny bedroom. Somewhere in that mess, Matt knew, were two blue hospital shirts—one of which he'd have to wear for work.

Matt held his nose and dug into the mess.

"Aha!" Matt whooped as he snatched a wrinkled shirt from the pile. He sniffed it, then made a face. The shirt stank!

Matt rummaged through the closet until he found a plastic jug of detergent. It was empty.

So was the bottle of dishwashing soap.

Finally, Matt found a spray can of furniture polish. He sprayed until a thick mist with the scent of fresh lemons—or, at least, its chemical equivalent—filled the apartment. Then he waved his shirt through the haze until it, too, smelled citrus fresh.

Then Matt found his gym bag, and began stuffing it with dirty laundry. There were lots and lots of clothes, and Matt was becoming more exasperated with every shove.

Just then, loud music blasted into the bedroom from the apartment next door. It was so loud the walls seemed to vibrate.

"I can't take this place anymore!" Matt cried, covering his ears.

Matt needed peace and quiet, lunch, and a washing machine. Fortunately, he knew where to find them.

"See ya later," Lucy called after student court was adjourned.

"Big day on Wednesday," Megan Reilley reminded her. "We'll be getting the judgments on all the cases we heard today."

"How could I forget?" Lucy replied. "We heard so many cases, I think half the school is waiting for a ruling."

"Great day today," Rod Dietle said, rushing by. He gave Lucy a thumbs-up.

"Yeah. Excellent!" Rod's friend Shelby Corman added.

Smiling, Lucy waved to them and walked to the parking lot. She found Mary leaning against the car.

"What are you doing here?" Lucy asked. "You're *never* finished with basketball practice before student court lets out."

When Mary spoke, her tone was evasive. "We had...a really short practice today," she said hesitantly, her face rigid.

"Why aren't you sweaty?" Lucy persisted.

Mary popped the passenger-side door open. "The coach just lectured us," Mary answered. "Gave us some things to think about, which I am doing as we speak."

Lucy studied her sister. Something was wrong—Lucy was certain. But Mary was a real pill when she didn't want to talk.

"Well," Mary barked, glaring. "Do you want to interrogate me like some perp in student court, or do you want to ride home with me?"

Lucy put her finger to her temple, pretending to think about this option. "Gee, Mary. How far is home from here?"

Mary rolled her eyes. "I don't know," she said. "Two, maybe three miles."

Lucy ran her fingers across her mouth. "My lips are sealed," she promised.

"I think student court is turning you into a lawyer," Mary observed.

"Is that so bad?" Lucy said as she fastened her seat belt.

Mary didn't reply. She just gunned the engine, threw the car into gear, and pulled out of the parking lot so fast that the tires squealed.

THREE

Simon heard his bedroom door open. Happy stirred at his side, but Simon lay still on the bed, pretending to sleep. The new issue of *Smart Money* magazine covered his face.

Simon detected a sigh and recognized it as Ruthie's. He continued to fake sleep, even when Ruthie climbed on the bed. Simon waited, hoping his sister would go away. Ruthie yawned loudly.

Curiosity got the better of him. Simon pulled the magazine away and sat up.

Ruthie was sprawled lengthwise across his bed. Her face was covered by an old issue of *Inside Kung Fu*. She faked a snore.

"What are you doing?" Simon demanded, ripping the magazine away.

"Resting my eyes?" Ruthie replied coyly.

Simon snorted.

"All right," Ruthie confessed. "I was keeping you company while you're busy being mad at Mom."

"Who said I'm mad at Mom?" Simon asked.

Ruthie rolled her eyes. "It's pretty obvious, I must say."

Simon sighed.

"I don't have the strength to stay mad at anyone for a long time," Ruthie continued.

Simon groaned and turned away from his sister just as the bedroom door swung open again.

Reverend Camden entered. "So," he said. "Quite a day, huh?" He sat down on the bed between Simon and Ruthie.

Simon sat up and was about to speak, then he glanced over at Ruthie.

"Don't let me stop you, Dad," Ruthie insisted. "Simon and I don't have any secrets."

"Not because I wouldn't mind having some," Simon shot back.

"Well, I never!" Ruthie said indignantly. The girl snatched both magazines and stomped out of the room. Happy yelped and followed Ruthie out the door.

"I guess Mom told you," Simon said when they were alone.

Reverend Camden nodded.

"The guys and I were just goofing around!" he said defensively. "Darryl burped, and before I knew it, my fingers were just kind of levitating around on their own."

Reverend Camden arched his eyebrow. "Both of them?"

"It just happened," Simon continued. "And all in about three seconds."

Simon sat back on the pillows. "Everybody thought it was funny at the time."

"Except your mother," Reverend Camden replied, "who picked those three seconds to drive up. Not to mention Principal Gordon."

"Okay," Simon said sheepishly. "I'll admit there was an element of bad timing at work."

"On the other hand," Reverend Camden offered, "you know your mom and I aren't fans of that particular gesture. It's disrespectful, rude, and obscene."

"I know," Simon said. "But I was just hanging out, being one of the guys."

"I get it," Reverend Camden said earnestly. "I really do. There is something great about hanging out with the guys. As long as being one of the guys doesn't mean that you are *swayed* by the guys."

Simon looked puzzled.

"For some reason, a lot of guys do really stupid things when they're with other guys," his father continued. "Things they wouldn't think of doing if they were alone."

"I get it," Simon said simply.

"It's just that I don't want you to ever lose your great ability to think and make decisions for yourself," Reverend Camden added.

"I won't," Simon promised.

A moment of silence passed.

"Your mother and I think a little break from the guys might be a good thing for you," Reverend Camden said gently.

Simon frowned. "I'm grounded?"

"Say, the weekend?"

"Sure, Dad," Simon whispered.

Reverend Camden kissed his son's head.

"Your mom and I love you, kiddo. You *and* your fingers. Just not in their upright and locked position, okay?"

Simon shrugged. Reverend Camden patted his arm and left.

"If Mom loves me so much," Simon said to the empty room, "how come I'm not her son anymore?

"How come I'm '*your* son'?" he whispered, repeating his mother's words. "'*Your* son.'"

Banished from Simon's room, Ruthie found her mother in the living room, feeding the twins and watching the local news.

Ruthie looked at Samuel and David. They both stared back at her and she shivered.

"These babies remind me of that painting," Ruthie said. "The one where the woman's eyes follow you around everywhere."

Mrs. Camden smiled. "The *Mona Lisa?*"

"Yeah!" Ruthie said. "That's the one."

"Well, honey," Mrs. Camden explained. "Their eyes are supposed to follow you around. They're *living* human beings."

Ruthie snorted.

"Well, it's creepy and I don't like it."

"I see," Mrs. Camden replied.

Matt opened the front door without knocking and came into the living room. He was wearing his hospital uniform and had an overstuffed gym bag slung over his shoulder.

Mrs. Camden smiled. "Hello, number one son!"

"We have so many sons now we have to *number* them!" Ruthie said, rolling her eyes.

Matt kissed his little sister. Ruthie wrinkled her nose.

"Why do you smell like furniture polish?"

Matt blushed with embarrassment. "I don't smell anything," he lied.

"What smells so lemony fresh?" Reverend Camden asked as he came downstairs.

Matt blushed again as his father pointed at him. "You, I think," Reverend Camden declared.

"New laundry detergent, I guess," Matt explained nervously.

"Anyway," he said, changing the subject. "I have an early shift at the hospital and I thought I'd swing by and say hi."

Mrs. Camden smiled knowingly. "Dinner will be served in a while. And you know where the washing machine is."

But Matt's eyes were on the television set, where local newswoman Carrie Chadwick was making a dramatic announcement.

Reverend Camden and his wife both turned their attention to the news broadcast when they heard the local high school mentioned.

"...In a decision that has taken the community by surprise, Jason Cleary, the girls' varsity basketball coach at Glenoak's Kennedy High School, has staged a lockout—of his own team..."

Just then, Mary and Lucy walked in.

Hearing the television news, Lucy faced her sister questioningly.

"...Despite the impressive win-loss record Cleary and his Lady Wildcats have amassed over the past few seasons, Coach Cleary has apparently canceled basketball for the girls of Glenoak for reasons unknown..."

Lucy leaned close to her sister. "How long were you going to keep this a secret?" she whispered.

When the segment ended, all eyes turned to Mary. But it was her father who broke the stunned silence.

"So," he said, his voice surprisingly calm. "How was *your* day, Mary?"

Simon was still lying in bed when Ruthie burst in, Happy yapping at her heels.

"Don't you ever knock?" he asked.

"If someone makes me," Ruthie said, her voice excited. "But you've got to come with me! We've got to go downstairs."

"I don't want to go," Simon replied. "Mom's mad at me and I just got grounded for the weekend. I've had an all-around bad day."

Ruthie tugged on his shirt.

"You've *got* to come," Ruthie insisted. "Mary's basketball coach just canceled a bunch of stuff or something and it was even on the TV news!"

"Huh?"

"No more basketball," Ruthie continued breathlessly. "And Mary just got home!"

"Well," Simon said. "If Mary's going to have a worse day than me, I don't want to seem unsupportive."

"I just want to see what happens!" Ruthie added as Simon followed her down the stairs.

*   *   *

"Okay," Mary explained, her tone angry. "We were all standing around in the hall waiting for the coach to show up and start practice. Instead, Coach Cleary locks us out of the gym!"

Mrs. Camden nodded. Matt frowned and said nothing. But Reverend Camden sensed there was more to the story.

"He can't do that, can he?" Mary demanded.

"Well, I..." But before her father could begin his thought, Mary was off again.

"Can't Coach Cleary be fired for something like this? I mean, the man works for someone. Who does he think he is? A dictator?"

Mary sat back in her chair, but her arms and legs wouldn't stay still.

"I've never heard of this happening before," Reverend Camden said quietly.

Lucy looked at Mary. "I'm not sure what the legal precedent is," she said. "It's not something we've come across in student court."

"The little lawyer speaks again," said Mary with a roll of her eyes. "Who cares about your stupid student court?"

"Mary!" Mrs. Camden cried. "Don't talk to Lucy like that."

"Sorry," Mary said to her sister. But she didn't sound sorry at all.

"This can't happen!" Mary continued. "This is my senior year. I already have a scholarship to play basketball. Coach Cleary is messing with people's futures. Somebody has to do something!"

Everyone stared in silence for a moment. Then a voice spoke up from the doorway: "Why did he lock you guys out?"

It was an innocent question that went right to the heart of the matter. All eyes turned to Simon.

"I was just curious," he said defensively.

"It's a good question," Lucy noted, looking hard at Mary.

But Mrs. Camden could clearly see the anger and frustration on Mary's face. She stepped in.

"Okay, everybody, break it up!" Mrs. Camden commanded. "There's nothing to see here, so everybody go back to your rooms."

Ruthie rolled her eyes. Simon hesitated at the living room door. Lucy refused to budge.

"GO!" Mrs. Camden barked. "We'll get back to you."

Matt put his hand on Simon and Ruthie's shoulders and guided them toward the doorway. Lucy reluctantly followed.

Simon sniffed the air, then asked one last question before Matt pushed him out of the room.

"Why do you smell like furniture polish?"

FOUR

Reverend Camden closed the living room door. Then he turned to face his wife and daughter.

"So?" he asked pointedly.

"So," Mary said after a frustrated sigh. "I heard that some of the girls' grades were slipping, and the coach wasn't going to let them play until their grades improved."

"And are you one of the 'some girls'?"

Mary looked down at her hands, which were twitching nervously. "I'm not sure," she admitted.

Then Mary looked up again; her eyes were burning with anger.

"This whole thing could mean no team and no season, which could mean no scholarship!" she cried. "Not to mention the major humiliation, which is already under way."

"We understand," Reverend Camden said. "Granted, the local news show isn't helping things, but in a couple of days, this whole matter will probably blow over."

Mary looked at her father hopefully.

"We want to talk to the coach," Mrs. Camden added. "We want to know what's going on."

"I just told you what was going on," Mary snapped.

"Yes, and beautifully," Mrs. Camden replied, her voice tense with strained patience. "But I still want to get a second opinion. I want to talk to the coach."

"I wish someone would," Mary said tersely. Then she made a hasty exit.

Reverend Camden and his wife could hear her footsteps as Mary ran to the attic room she shared with Lucy.

"I don't want to jump to the worst-case scenario," Mrs. Camden said. "But we can't swing college tuition for Mary without getting some kind of scholarship help, can we?"

Reverend Camden shook his head. "No," he whispered. "No, we can't."

*   *   *

When Mary got to the top of the stairs, Matt was waiting for her.

"You decided to do the senior year surf and coast, didn't you?" he said accusingly.

Matt followed her up the second flight of stairs and into her room.

"Did you really think no one was going to notice if your grades took the plunge?"

Mary plopped down onto her bed and tried to put a pillow over her head. Matt pulled it away.

"Just what kind of disciplined, mature person decides to coast through their senior year?" he demanded.

"The kind with a scholarship!" Mary screamed. "But you wouldn't know what that's like because *you* couldn't get one."

That hurt, Matt thought sourly. He lashed back at his sister. "Listen, Mary. Mom just had two babies, Dad just had a heart attack, and now this. Don't you think Mom and Dad have enough going on without having to worry about you and the stuff you've been letting slide?"

With no comeback handy, Mary muttered something incomprehensible.

"You're supposed to be the oldest," Matt continued. "How can Mom and Dad trust you to keep an eye on everyone else when you can't even keep an eye on your-self?"

"Oh, boy," Mary sighed, finally thinking of a response that might shut Matt up. "Here comes another lecture about what it means to be the oldest. How many times am I going to have to hear this stuff?"

Matt looked into Mary's eyes. "Until you get it right."

Mary threw a pillow at him, but Matt snatched it out of the air. Then she put both of her hands on Matt's chest and pushed him through the doorway.

"Get out of my room!" she demanded.

"Not until you listen to reason," Matt replied, fighting her.

"Go away!" Mary cried even louder. "And take your lemony scent with you!"

Then she slammed the door in Matt's face.

Simon heard the loud voices coming from Mary's room. For a moment he was tempted to listen, but decided it was none of his business. He'd gotten himself into enough trouble today. He didn't need any more.

Ruthie pushed her way into his room before he had the chance to close the door.

"What are *we* doing?" Ruthie asked.

"We?" Simon shot back.

"Mom and Dad are busy. Lucy is studying. Matt is fighting with Mary. Which leaves *you*."

Simon surrendered to the inevitable. "Come on in," he sighed.

"So what are *we* doing?" Ruthie repeated.

"Nothing," he said sadly. "Mom and Dad said I can't hang out with the guys."

"You can hang out with me."

"It's not the same," Simon said. "You're not a guy. My friends and I are guys. I even have the chest hair to prove it."

Ruthie looked doubtful. "Let's see."

Simon pulled down the neck of his sweatshirt. "See."

Ruthie squinted and looked closely. Then she pulled at something on Simon's chest.

"Ouch!" he cried.

"Sorry," Ruthie said. "I thought it was sweatshirt fuzz."

"Well, it wasn't!" Simon shot back testily. "It was a chest hair and it was the only one I had. Now it's gone."

"If you're such a guy, grow more!" Ruthie said. "Dad and Matt can't stop

growing hair. They're like gorillas or something."

"I will, I will," Simon said. "When I feel
like it. Right now I'm...pacing myself."

"Oh, sure," Ruthie nodded. "And with
or without chest hair, I can be as good a
guy as your stupid guy friends."

"Half the stuff we guys do would probably make you throw up," Simon shot
back.

"If I can watch the twins eat, nothing
will make me throw up," Ruthie insisted.

"Oh, no?" Simon stepped up to Ruthie
and burped in her face.

"Lame," Ruthie declared.

"Well, watch this!" Simon put his right
hand under his armpit and made a disgust-
ing honking noise.

Ruthie looked at him, then leaned in
confidently.

"I don't have to do the fake kind," she
informed him.

Simon's nose wrinkled when the odor
hit him. Happy yelped and fled the room.

After dinner, Lucy and Reverend Camden
were on cleanup duty.

He rinsed the last of the dishes and
handed them to Lucy, who placed them in

slots on the top rack of the dishwasher. She added cleanser and closed the door.

When the dishwashing cycle began, Lucy and her father sat down at the kitchen table. He poured them each a tall glass of cold milk.

"How were things in court today?" Reverend Camden asked.

"Sometimes I think most of the school hates me because I'm acting like a lawyer or something." Lucy sighed.

"I see."

"It's only student court," Lucy added. "But it feels important. I know that sounds dumb."

Reverend Camden shook his head.

"There's nothing dumb about it," he said. "In some ways, what you do is similar to what I do."

"You think so?" asked Lucy.

"People come to me," he began, "and they tell me what they're thinking, or feeling, or doing, and I listen. Then I give them my perspective. I tell them the possible consequences of their beliefs and behaviors."

Lucy sat in silence a moment. "And that's like student court?"

"Don't you think that anyone you saw in court left with a new perspective on themselves or their behavior?" Reverend Camden asked.

"I honestly don't know," Lucy said. Yet, her dad's words made her think. She took her student court service seriously, but she'd never thought about it as something that could help people the same way her dad did.

"Well," he said. "All you can do is try to provide a different perspective. After that, it's up to the person and their free will to see what'll happen next."

Lucy nodded.

"It may not seem like much," Reverend Camden concluded, "but it *is* important, Lucy. It really is."

Lucy smiled. "I guess we have something in common, then, huh, Dad?"

"We have a lot of somethings in common," Reverend Camden replied with a note of pride. "This is just one of them."

"I guess your job is a lot harder than most people think."

"Well, I admit, there are days," Reverend Camden said with a smile. "But I try to remember that old saying."

"Saying?"

"We have to be the change we wish to see in the world."

"Wow," Lucy whispered. "Is that from the Bible or one of those saint guys?"

Her father winked. "It's from Gandhi."

Lucy nodded again. Gandhi was one of her heroes. His courageous philosophy of nonviolence had influenced many great leaders, including Martin Luther King. "Well, I'll give it a try."

"Just a little fatherly advice," Reverend Camden added. "It's easier to *say* than to *do*."

Lucy laughed. "Amen to that!"

FIVE

Instead of returning to his noisy apartment, Matt drove back to the Camden house after his work shift at the hospital ended. He hadn't finished his laundry yet, and figured that no one else was going to finish it for him.

But there was another reason for going home, Matt knew.

Things were spiraling out of control, and Matt felt he had to help. His family needed him, and, for Matt, family always came first. That's what being a man—and a Camden—was all about.

As he pulled into the driveway, the house appeared quiet. The kitchen lights were off. He went in through the back door and paused in the kitchen to grab a snack, saying a silent thanks for the stocked pantry and full gallon of milk in the fridge.

With his half-eaten peanut butter and jelly sandwich in hand, Matt headed upstairs.

At the top of the stairs, the door to Ruthie's room flew open and his little sister walked out. Matt blinked and his jaw dropped when he saw her.

Is that Ruthie?

Matt swallowed a bite of sandwich. "What are you supposed to be?"

"One of the guys," Ruthie answered proudly. She accented her words with a boyish toss of her head.

"Is that outfit you're wearing Simon's idea?"

"He thinks I'm not man enough to be one of the guys," Ruthie explained. "But I wanted to show him he was wrong."

Matt shook his head sadly.

"Hey, Matt!" Ruthie asked. "What does this mean?"

Matt nearly choked on his sandwich when Ruthie made a very rude and vulgar gesture—with the fingers of both hands!

Simon almost jumped out of his socks when Matt burst through his door with

Ruthie under one arm. She squealed with delight at the attention she was getting, even as she was struggling to get free.

Matt dumped Ruthie on the bed. She bounced playfully, scattering Simon's magazines.

"Ruthie's just been showing me some of the 'guy stuff' you've taught her," Matt said.

Simon snorted. "Like she ever listens to me."

"No, but apparently she does *watch* you."

Simon studied the girl's outfit.

"So, she's dressed in my clothes."

"And she imitates your gestures," Matt said meaningfully. "*All* of them."

"All right," Simon relented. "Just stop the witch-hunt, okay."

"What happened?"

"I was messing around with the guys after school and it just…happened."

"It?" Matt arched his eyebrow.

"The finger thing."

"So, how much trouble are you in?" Matt demanded.

"Mom saw me," Simon continued uneasily. "And Principal Gordon saw me—"

"And *I* saw him!" Ruthie interrupted.

"He kind of wiggled his rear end around when he did it, too. It was so cute."

"Shut up, please!" Simon pleaded.

"Smooth move, ace," Matt observed.

"Like *you* never did it!" Simon shot back.

"*If* I ever did anything like that," Matt said patiently. "And that's a big *if*. But if I did that, I sure wouldn't stand in front of school waving it around like I was trying to land planes."

"There was an unfortunate element of bad timing involved."

"There was an unfortunate element of bad *judgment* involved, too," Matt added. "Better, wiser, more mature judgment would have told you to scope things out first."

"You know how it is," Simon whined. "I got caught up in the moment. It doesn't make me a criminal, it just makes me a *guy*."

"The kind of guy you're turning Ruthie into?"

The little girl giggled.

"I get it, believe me," Matt added. "But you know, when I got older, I learned that being a guy is one thing and being a *man* is another."

"But—"

Matt cut him off. "That guy stuff has nothing to do with being a man. A man stands up for himself and the people he loves. He looks out for and protects them. And he takes responsibility for his actions."

"That's it?" Simon said dubiously. "That can't be right. It can't be that simple! There has to be more to being a man than that."

"It sounds easier than it is," Matt responded indignantly. "Believe me."

"Oh, I'm sure," Simon replied with a hint of sarcasm. "But in the meantime, you got to have fun doing all that guy stuff with your friends until you got older and figured out it was stupid."

"That's not—" Matt tried to break in, but this time Simon was on a roll, and wouldn't let his brother get in a word.

"Thanks to you," Simon cried, "I know *now*, seven years too early. And now, nothing will be the same, because every time I go to burp, every time I think, 'Hey, make a face at Darryl,' a little voice in my head that sounds an awful lot like *you* will say 'that's stupid.'"

Simon stuck his hand under his armpit and tried to make a rude noise. But his heart wasn't in it. The magic was gone.

"See?" Simon cried accusingly. "Ruined."

He sighed, then looked up at his brother. "But thank you, Matt. Thank you for making me a *man*."

Ruthie looked at Matt, her arms folded.

"Yeah," she said with a frown. "Thank you."

"Look," Matt said. "I'm sorry if I ruined your childhood, but I have an idea."

"Yeah, what's that?"

"Why don't you come over and hang with me and the guys at my apartment tomorrow," Matt suggested. "We'll watch the football game and eat some pizza..."

"I don't know," Simon replied, hiding his interest. "I'll get back to you."

"Ditto," Ruthie said, excited by the idea.

"By the way," Matt said on his way out. "That under the arm...ah..."

"Honking?" Simon replied.

"Oh, yeah," Matt nodded. "Mom hates that other word."

"But she can live with honking," Simon added.

"But only as a word, not an activity."

"Your point?" Simon demanded.

"That honking thing you do needs

work…It's pretty lame, you know."

"I'm sorry," Simon replied, his sarcasm turned up full blast. "Do you have other dreams of mine you wish to dash? Shouldn't you be telling the twins about war, taxes, and prostates?"

"You'll thank me one day," Matt declared. He smiled smugly and stuck his hand in his armpit. What emerged was the loudest honk Simon had ever heard.

When he was gone, Ruthie turned to Simon. "That was awesome," she exclaimed.

Simon rolled over on the bed and put a pillow over his head.

"Do you think Simon's right?" Mrs. Camden asked.

Reverend Camden pulled the blanket up around David and Samuel and kissed the twins before he turned to his wife.

"Simon is almost *never* right," he observed.

"This is serious," Mrs. Camden insisted. "Do you think Simon's right, that I don't know what 'guy stuff' is because I'm not a guy?"

"Well," Reverend Camden said after a pause. "Guys *are* wired differently, but you know that. And Matt doesn't seem to have suffered because he was raised by a dad and a mom who wasn't a guy."

Mrs. Camden laughed.

"You have to understand," he continued. "Simon was just acting—"

"Like a guy, I know."

"No," her husband replied. "Simon was acting like a thirteen-year-old who was embarrassed in front of his buddies."

He hugged his wife. "Simon'll get over it."

David gurgled and began to cry. Mrs. Camden rolled her eyes. "*Now* you want to eat," she said in exasperation.

She bent low and lifted the infant from his crib. But before she could put the bottle to David's mouth, the phone rang.

"I'll get it," Mrs. Camden said, thrusting the bottle and the baby into her husband's arms.

As Mrs. Camden ran to get the phone, Mary drifted by the room.

"How about a little help?" Reverend Camden called. Mary took David out of his arms. Soon the boy was chewing on his bottle.

"Why can't I do that?" Reverend Camden wondered.

Mrs. Camden returned.

"Who was on the phone?"

"It was Ms. Russell," she informed them. "Apparently, there's been quite a response to the team lockout. So much response that the coach had to take his phone off the hook."

"That explains why I couldn't get through to him," Reverend Camden said.

"Well, the upshot is that Ms. Russell has scheduled a group meeting for tomorrow afternoon."

"Good!" Mary cried, startling the baby. "You guys are going, right?"

"We already have a meeting with Simon's principal," the reverend said. "But we'll be going to your meeting, too."

Mrs. Camden nodded. "We want to hear what the coach and Ms. Russell have to say."

"You won't believe it when you do," Mary replied.

Mary departed, happy that the meeting was set. She passed Matt, who stuck his head in his parents' bedroom.

"Sorry for interrupting," he said. "Would it be okay if I stayed here overnight? My apartment is hugely loud."

"Of course," his mother replied.

"I just need a little peace and quiet to think about things," Matt continued.

"Things," Reverend Camden's ears perked up. "Anything we can help you with?"

Matt shrugged. "Nah. It's a little bit of everything—classes, life, maybe moving back home. That kind of thing."

"I don't think we can feed another mouth," Mrs. Camden said when Matt was gone.

"We'll manage," Reverend Camden assured her. But the truth was, he needed some assurance himself.

SIX

The next day, Simon and his parents headed to Simon's school. They had an appointment to keep at Principal Gordon's office.

There was a moment of awkward silence when they arrived and settled in. Then Ms. Gordon folded her hands on her desk and spoke.

"I'm pretty sure you won't be surprised to hear that Simon's behavior is considered unacceptable at this school," she said.

"It's also considered unacceptable at home," Mrs. Camden added.

Sitting between his mother and father, Simon swallowed nervously. His heart was beating so fast he thought his chest would explode.

"We think that a three-day suspension from school is in order," Ms. Gordon said. "It's the standard consequence."

Reverend Camden blinked in surprise. Mrs. Camden frowned. Simon figured his parents would be really furious with him now. But, to his surprise, his dad spoke up—to *defend* him.

"I'm not advocating what he did," Reverend Camden said, "but three days' suspension? That seems like a little bit of an overreaction."

"Not at all," Ms. Gordon explained. "Simon's behavior falls in the category of harassing, gang, or indecent gestures."

Simon could feel his mother tensing beside him. If there was one thing he knew, it was when his mom was about ready to blow her stack. And she looked like she was just about there.

"Simon is a good student with a good record at school," Mrs. Camden said through clenched teeth. "And as far as his gesture goes, it was rude and vulgar, but nothing more or less than that."

Ms. Gordon sat back, her face rigid. It was obvious she wasn't buying Mrs. Camden's argument.

"Simon has apologized for his actions,"

Mrs. Camden continued. "And he is not, and will never be a harasser, a gang member, or indecent."

Ms. Gordon sighed. "I'm sorry. But there is no room for latitude. We are talking about school policy."

"No, we are *not* talking about school policy," Mrs. Camden returned. "If you had been listening at all, you'd know that we were talking about *my son!*"

Simon, who had been trying to disappear into his chair, sat up when he heard the words "my son."

"Come on," she told Simon and her husband as she jumped to her feet. "We're going."

Simon watched his mother storm out of the room and his father slowly rise to his feet.

"I'm sorry, Reverend," Ms. Gordon said. "Please talk to your wife."

"Don't worry, I will," he told the principal. "I'll tell her that she was *right.*"

The trio met again in the parking lot.

Simon felt miserable as he climbed into the minivan's backseat.

"Hey," said his mother, spying him in the rearview mirror. "Are you okay?"

Simon shrugged, trying to hold back tears.

"We'll figure something out," Mrs. Camden said. "If nothing else, we'll have three days of quality time."

"It's not that," Simon said. "It's just that I thought you didn't *want* me anymore."

"For what?" she said incredulously.

"For your *son*," Simon replied.

"Where did you get that silly idea?" Mrs. Camden demanded, stunned.

"I overheard you tell Dad that *his* son did this and *his* son did that a bunch of times," Simon whispered.

Mrs. Camden shot her husband a meaningful look. He got the message.

"The front tire looked a little low," Reverend Camden said awkwardly. "And, uh, that can't be good. Think I'd better check it out."

He left his wife and son alone.

"Simon," Mrs. Camden said after a quiet moment. "I didn't mean it that way. The words…they just came out."

"That's what happened with my fingers. They just came out, too," said Simon. "I guess we have something in common."

Mrs. Camden smiled. "I guess we do. I

think I was upset with you because the gesture is just so—"

"Vulgar and indecent?"

"Yeah." Mrs. Camden nodded. "But it is also ordinary."

"Ordinary?"

"Sure," Mrs. Camden explained. "The people who make that gesture aren't smart or clever enough to think of something better to do."

Simon wasn't sure he understood.

"I remember after I'd just had you in the hospital," Mrs. Camden continued. "I was holding you and looking at you and thinking how amazing it was that I could do this extraordinary thing."

"Really?" asked Simon.

"And you, Simon Camden, have grown up to be one of the most extraordinary people I know. So, I guess, even if it was just normal guy stuff, I was disappointed to see you doing something so ordinary as use your finger."

"I'm sorry, Mom," he said.

"Me, too." Mrs. Camden sighed. "For my words, for everything. I love you."

Outside, Reverend Camden was sitting on the bumper of the minivan. He risked a peek into the van's interior and saw Simon hugging his mother.

The reverend smiled. At least *one* family crisis was coming to an end.

Meanwhile, at Glenoak's Kennedy High School, all eyes were on Mary Camden as she moved through the halls.

Mary, along with the other members of the Lady Wildcat varsity basketball team, were the objects of curiosity and gossip. Mary didn't like it. Not one bit.

As she pushed through the crowd, Mary could hear people whispering. Although she couldn't make out their words, she could imagine what they were saying.

Isn't that Mary Camden, star player and captain of the basketball team?

Not anymore. The season's canceled. Mary is just like everyone else, now. Just another ordinary senior...

When she got to her locker, Mary found her teammates Corey and Karen waiting for her. Corey smiled when she spotted Mary.

"Did you see the story about the team lockout on the news last night?" Corey asked.

They were joined by Danny and Greg,

two star players on the boys' basketball team.

"We heard what happened," Danny said, his voice angry. "What is Coach Cleary thinking? You guys are tied for first place, with the best record in this school's history!"

"Yeah," Greg added. "You got a shot at the league championship! Why would he lock you out?"

"It was some grade thing," Mary explained.

"Grades!" Greg shot back. "If you guys are meeting the league's minimum grade-point average, that's all that matters."

The girls looked at Greg with new interest.

"Really?" Corey gasped.

"Sure," Greg continued. "That kind of information is in the league bylaws. Maybe Coach Cleary should *read* them."

"Where could we get a copy of these bylaws?" Mary demanded.

"Somebody at the league office should know," Danny shrugged. "Give them a call."

Oh, we will," Corey said.

"Hang in there," Greg said, heading for class.

Mary turned to Corey with her hand out. "Got a quarter for the telephone?"

Just down the hall, Lucy Camden found herself flanked by two friends, each one trying to find out what she knew about the lockout.

"I heard that a couple of the girls failed drug tests and that's why Cleary locked them out," Rod announced.

"What?" Lucy cried, horrified.

"I heard that the whole team was into buying tests and papers and stuff," Shelby said.

Lucy shook her head in disbelief. "You've got to be kidding!"

Rod pulled Lucy aside. "I also heard that a couple of the girls are really Russian ringers brought over to help win the championship."

"That's just nuts," said Lucy.

"No it isn't," Rod insisted. "With the collapse of the Russian economy, it makes sense."

"On what planet?" returned Lucy.

"Well, if *you* know so much, Ms. Student Court, let us in on the secret," Rod demanded.

Lucy considered whether to reveal what she knew. It was a private matter—between the coach and his team. On the other hand, if she didn't set her friends straight they would continue spreading these stupid, far-out rumors.

If I tell them the truth, Lucy thought, *maybe they'll be satisfied and just shut up about the whole thing.*

"You can't tell anyone," Lucy whispered, looking around. "But the reason for the lockout was that their grades fell."

Rod blinked. "That's it? You've got to be kidding!"

"Man," Shelby said, disappointed. "And I thought if it was on the news, it had to be something really good—I mean, you know, really *bad.*"

"Yeah," Rod said. "The woman on TV made it sound totally juicy."

"Well," Lucy whispered. "Don't tell anybody. I promised Mary I wouldn't say anything."

"No problem," Rod said.

"You've got it," Shelby promised.

"Thanks," Lucy called over her shoulder as she sped off to class.

When she was gone, Rod and Shelby

looked at each other and shrugged. Then they turned to the very next group of students coming down the hall and began to spread the juiciest gossip they'd heard in weeks.

SEVEN

Home sweet home, Matt thought bitterly as he unlocked the door to his apartment. He could already hear the loud music blasting out of his neighbor's apartment.

When he swung open the door, he found Shana sitting cross-legged on the couch.

"John let me in," she explained. "When I found out you weren't here I got worried."

"I know we had this study date and I'm sorry I'm late," Matt said, dropping his gym bag full of freshly laundered clothes. "Something bad came up and I had to keep an eye on the twins for my parents."

Just then, the volume on the neighbor's stereo doubled.

"I can't take much more of living like

this!" Matt cried over the noise. He pounded on the wall with his fists. The volume went down, but the music was still too loud.

"Is everything okay?" Shana asked.

"Not exactly."

"What's wrong with—"

"Everything!" Matt replied before Shana could even finish the question. "Mary's coach has temporarily canceled the season because of the team's—and Mary's—bad grades!"

"Oh, Matt."

"Yeah," he agreed. "And Mary is too stubborn to see that coasting through senior year puts her scholarship in jeopardy."

Matt sat down next to Shana.

"There's more," he said. "Simon got caught giving the finger at school, got suspended, and then Ruthie gave the finger to me!"

Shana couldn't hide her amusement.

"She didn't know what she was doing!" Matt added. "She asked me what it meant."

"What did you tell her?"

"I told her to ask my dad."

"Smooth move." Shana laughed.

"I'd laugh, too," Matt said, "except that

my dad just had a heart attack, and my brother and sisters have all lost their minds."

Shana put her arms around Matt. "You're a good brother. But a brother can only do so much. Your mom and dad can handle things."

"Can they?" Matt demanded. "My father's heart attack proves there are limits to how much he can handle, and nobody but me seems to understand that."

The front door opened and John came in.

"Hey, what's going on?" he said.

"Nothing much," said Shana. "Matt was just pounding on the wall again."

"Good! We're going to have to have a talk with that guy."

John took a closer look at Matt. "What's wrong, man?"

"Things are out of control at my house," Matt said. "And with my dad's condition and all, I'm thinking about moving back home."

John's jaw dropped.

"Did your parents ask you to move back?" John asked after a moment of shocked silence.

"Uh...no. But you know them," Matt

said quickly. "They'd never ask. No matter what they were going through."

"I understand," John said. "But I can't handle the rent on this place alone, so I hope you'll give me a little notice when you're done 'thinking' about it."

With that, John wheeled around and strode out of the room. Matt heard John's bedroom door shut a little too loudly.

"What's his problem?" Matt asked, feeling his own anger rising. "If I do this, I'll be doing it for my parents. Not for myself."

Shana looked him in the eye. "Are you sure?"

"Absolutely."

Across town, television news reporter Carrie Chadwick was waiting in front of Kennedy High for the school day to end.

Coach Cleary's lockout was big news, and the reporter wasn't going to let the story die. Her coverage had already boosted the ratings of the local news show.

Carrie Chadwick knew she had to stay on top of things if she didn't want this story stolen from under her. And she had to keep things lively, even if it meant stirring the pot a little.

That's why I'm here, Carrie thought as

she approached the school's front steps. *To make sure something happens.*

At that moment, Carrie Chadwick heard the final bell ring. She keyed her mike and motioned for her cameraman to stand by.

"Greg was right!" Mary cried as she rushed up to her friends.

After classes had let out, some of the Lady Wildcat players had gathered at the base of the high school's front steps.

"All the league requires is that a player have a grade-point average of 2.0 or higher to be eligible to play!" Mary explained to her teammates.

Corey, Elaine, Maggie, and Karen stared at her.

"That's all?" Maggie asked. "Just 2.0!"

Mary nodded. She knew that her grades had slipped, but not *that* far! And she could see from her friends' expressions that their grades were above the base requirement, too.

"Then where does Coach Cleary get off—"

But Karen's angry question was cut short when the coach himself appeared. He walked past them with a nod and strode right up the school's front steps.

Carrie Chadwick and her cameraman rushed him immediately. A microphone was quickly thrust under Coach Cleary's nose.

"Coach Cleary!" the woman shouted over the noise of the students. "Will you answer a couple of questions?"

Coach Cleary tried to push past the newswoman and go inside the school. But Carrie Chadwick blocked his way.

"How about a comment on the unprecedented lockout of a team by its own coach?" she pressed.

But the coach wasn't talking. He ducked past the cameraman and entered the school—where no cameras were permitted.

Frustrated, Carrie Chadwick scanned the area for someone else to interview. It didn't take her long to spot the bright red varsity jackets of the Lady Wildcats at the base of the school's front steps.

With a quick flick of her wrist, Carrie Chadwick motioned her crew to follow as she approached the girls.

"Hey," Carrie said cheerfully, "I hope I'm not interrupting."

Mary avoided the woman's gaze, not

sure she wanted to air her differences with the coach on television.

"I'm Carrie Chadwick from Channel Eight news," she continued. "And though it looks like the Lady Wildcats may be locked out for the rest of the season, it also looks like you are all still a team."

Her flattery worked. Both Elaine and Corey nodded enthusiastically. "You better believe it," Maggie said, raising her fist.

Carrie Chadwick smiled. She could smell a story here. "After the big meeting today, the coach and the school promised to issue a statement," the reporter continued, "but it will be an *official* statement."

The newswoman paused. When she spoke again, her voice was oozing with sincerity.

"The problem with an *official* statement is that it doesn't always tell the *whole* story...If you know what I mean."

It was Maggie who took the bait.

"Oh, yeah," Maggie said with a nod. "There's another side the school doesn't care to hear."

"Coach Cleary didn't even have the right to do what he did!" Elaine cried passionately.

"You're kidding," Carrie Chadwick

responded with false surprise.

"Not according to league rules, anyway," Maggie added, grabbing Mary's notes.

Carrie Chadwick flicked her wrist, and the camera focused on the Lady Wildcats.

Mary kept her eyes to the ground. She didn't like what Coach Cleary was doing, but she knew that involving the media was not a smart way to deal with the problem.

The other Wildcats didn't see it that way, and Mary stuck with her friends because of the loyalty she felt for her team.

She assured herself that it was the right thing to do.

EIGHT

"Come on!" Reverend Camden called up to the second floor. "We're going to be late."

Mrs. Camden rushed down the stairs. "Okay, kids," she said. "We're going."

"Don't worry about us," Lucy insisted. "We'll be fine."

"Yeah, Mom, the twins are in good hands," agreed Simon.

Suddenly, Ruthie stood up, stuck her hand under her arm and made a loud honking sound.

"Ignore her," Simon said. "She's getting ready for guys' night at Matt's."

"How is that?" Mrs. Camden asked.

"By being one of the guys!" Ruthie explained, honking again.

Lucy shook her head. "Under-the-arm

honking is not a *guy* thing!"

Simon was shocked. "It is too!"

"It is not," Lucy said. "Anybody can do it." To prove her point, Lucy thrust her hand under her shirt and let loose with the loudest honk Simon had heard since Matt's performance.

Mrs. Camden's jaw dropped. She was about to speak, but her husband stopped her. "This can wait."

Mrs. Camden sighed. "We shouldn't be gone long," she told Lucy. "I'm sure this meeting will clear everything up."

Inside the high school, the scene was chaotic. Reverend Camden and his wife weaved their way through a noisy throng of people.

Mrs. Camden eyed the crowd. "The report on the news had something to do with this huge turnout, I'm sure," she said.

Students, parents, teachers, and other faculty members had filled the lobby outside the gym's main entrance. The meeting was closed to everyone but the team and their parents, but that didn't stop a curious crowd from showing up to see what they could overhear from the gym's double doors.

Reverend Camden spotted Mary, who was already seated in the bleachers. Most of her teammates—and their parents— were there, too, waiting for the assembly to begin.

"Over here!" Mary called. Reverend and Mrs. Camden reached her a moment later.

Corey's father, in the row behind them, rose and shook Reverend Camden's hand.

"Hello, Reverend," he said jovially. "We'll get this straightened out. Coach Cleary is in trouble now."

"How do you figure?" Mrs. Camden asked.

"Didn't you see?" Corey's mother broke in. "The Channel Eight news van is in the parking lot. Coach Cleary wouldn't dare continue this lockout with the media watching."

Mrs. Camden frowned, unconvinced.

"Hi, Annie!"

Mrs. Camden saw Maggie's mother sitting with her daughter, who had a sour expression on her pretty face.

"Good to see you," Mrs. Camden called. "And you, too, Maggie."

But Maggie didn't answer. Her eyes were locked on the podium at the front of the gym. She was completely ignoring everyone and everything else.

"What's with Maggie?" Mrs. Camden asked Mary.

"Her scholarship is on hold," Mary explained. "She—"

Before Mary could say anything more, Principal Russell, Coach Cleary, and Robert Kent, the director of the school's athletic events, called the assembly to order.

"I'm happy you have all chosen to attend this meeting," Ms. Russell began. "I know you all have a lot of questions about Coach Cleary's decision. And I know that the news reports haven't told the real story."

She turned to the coach, who stood behind her waiting his turn to speak.

"Why don't we let Coach Cleary explain things," Ms. Russell concluded. "Then he'll answer your questions, one at a time."

Cleary approached the parents and began to dole out folders. Mary winced when she saw they were the team's academic reports.

After the parents received their daughters' reports, Coach Cleary took his place behind the podium.

"I'm not sure how much or what version of the story your daughters told you," he began. "But you are holding your daughters' most recent academic progress reports in your hands."

The coach paused. "I want you to look at them for a moment."

The only sound that could be heard was the shuffling of papers, and a ripple of distressed whispers.

"Now I'm sure you don't track your kids' grades on a weekly basis," Coach Cleary continued. "But *I* do. And I'll bet more than a few of you will be surprised by what you see."

Mary's parents scanned her report. They didn't look happy. Reverend Camden turned to Mary.

"You weren't *sure* if your grades were slipping?" he whispered, his voice shaking with barely controlled anger. "How could you not know?"

"Let me point out that despite repeated warnings and offers of academic assistance," Coach Cleary continued, "the girls have allowed their grades to slide."

Elaine's mother spoke out. "My daughter's grades are *my* business, not yours," she cried. "You're just her basketball coach."

"That's true," Coach Cleary said, nodding. "And as their coach, I care enough about them to do what is best. And making them take their schoolwork seriously is what's best."

Karen's father rose to speak.

"Is it true that the girls have met the basketball league's eligibility requirements?" he demanded.

"Yes. But the league's requirements are 2.0, and that's substandard," the coach argued. "Especially for these girls."

"Who are you to say?" an angry father called out. "Basketball is the only shot my kid has at a scholarship. And a scholarship is the only way she's going to college. How dare you take that opportunity away from her!"

Coach Cleary held his ground.

"How dare your *daughter* throw that opportunity away?" he demanded. "And where do you think your daughter is going to get a scholarship with grades like that?"

"The guys' team doesn't do this," someone shouted from the audience.

"Then your daughter should try out for the guys' team," Cleary shot back.

A few people laughed, but the tension was far from gone.

"No!" another parent shouted. "But you should be fired. And we should sue for discrimination."

Principal Russell stepped up to the podium. "No one wants to see this situation come to that," she said. "But everyone seems to be forgetting that the girls are dictating the schedule here."

"How's that!" Corey's father demanded.

"When they bring their grades back up, practice will start again."

More angry voices cried out.

"Until that happens," Ms. Russell declared, "the school is going to support Coach Cleary in his decision. The lockout will continue."

Reverend Camden finally decided to speak up. "Mary Camden is our daughter," he called out.

Everyone in the room quieted down when they heard the reverend's voice.

"She's a senior captain, and was the first freshman to make varsity in years," he continued. "She has overcome injuries and knee surgery to keep playing this game.

"As hard as she's worked and sweated through everything, so have we."

Mary smiled hopefully.

"Our commitment to this game may be

different from hers, but it's no less invested," Reverend Camden declared.

All the parents in the room seemed to nod in agreement with the reverend's words.

Then he locked eyes with Mary.

"Did you know your grades were this bad?" he asked loud enough for everyone to hear.

Mary hesitated, then nodded.

"Is there something you could have done to stop them from slipping?"

Mary shrugged.

"And did Coach Cleary tell you what would happen if your grades continued to slip?" her father continued relentlessly.

Mary nodded again, her face red.

Reverend Camden turned his eyes to the podium. "Then for now," he said, "we're going to respect this lockout."

"What?" Mary cried.

Mrs. Camden leaned over and whispered into Mary's ear. "I'm sorry, kiddo. Your coach didn't blow it. *You* did."

Carrie Chadwick stood before Glenoak's Kennedy High School. The cameraman had been instructed to frame it dramatically behind her.

Unlike the usual Friday night, which featured a Lady Wildcat basketball game, the school was dark and the parking lot empty.

"At issue," began the reporter, as she gazed into the TV camera, "is the distance between the classroom and the gymnasium. It is a distance not measured in feet or inches, but in attitudes. The questions are these: How much of a student athlete is *student* and how much is *athlete?* And who should decide what standards should be?"

Carrie Chadwick moved, so the camera could take in the darkened school.

"These are tough questions, sure," she continued. "But they are questions that have to be answered here in Glenoak where, after a probing investigation by this reporter, we've learned that school officials and a cadre of parents have decided to honor Coach Jason Cleary's girls' varsity basketball team lockout when it was revealed during a closed meeting with parents that the lockout came as a result of the students' declining academic performance."

The cameraman panned in, so that the deadly quiet school seemed like the center of the universe.

"Some in the community have cheered the coach's decision. Others have cried 'foul' and accuse Coach Cleary of overstepping the bounds of his position, calling for his immediate termination and promising further legal action if the ban is not lifted."

Carrie stepped back into the shot.

"In the meantime," she continued, "Coach Cleary and the Lady Wildcats, along with the rest of the community, are taking a timeout in the first half of what promises to be an intense match."

The camera pulled back to a full-body shot of the newswoman. Carrie Chadwick was wearing workout gear and sneakers. One hand held a microphone, the other hand, a basketball.

"I'll be keeping my eye on the ball as this story develops."

With that, the newswoman tried to dribble the ball. She lost control, and the ball bounced out of camera range.

"Cut!" the producer cried.

"They didn't see me drop the ball, did they?" Carrie demanded when the cameras were shut off.

The producer stared at the reporter.

"Basketball doesn't have matches," he

pointed out, "it only has quarters, halves, and games."

Carrie Chadwick stamped her foot, but the producer shook his head. It had been a long night, and he wasn't about to retape the segment.

"This is a wrap!" he called, throwing his headset into the van. "Let's get back to the studio."

NINE

That evening, things were quiet at the Camdens'.

"Too quiet!" Ruthie declared.

Simon nodded. "Mary's not yelling, door slamming, or even stomping around. That's not good, not good at all."

"Nope," Ruthie agreed. "Not good at all."

They had been sitting in Simon's room, reading magazines and watching Happy snooze—until the silence finally got to them.

"Mary is up to something," Simon said. "I'm sure of it."

"Mom and Dad don't have a clue!" Ruthie added. "They are too busy taking care of the Children of the Corn."

"Stop calling them that," Simon insisted. "It's from a horror novel. Once they're old enough to figure that out, it'll warp their little minds."

"I'll stop *saying* it," Ruthie replied. "But I can't stop *thinking* it. They *are* the Children of the Corn! So perfect and alike it's creepy. Just look at them—"

"You know, you might be right about Mom and Dad being too busy," Simon interrupted. "But just because they're a little distracted, that doesn't mean they should stop watching Mary."

"Like a hawk," Ruthie added.

"Hang on!" Simon cried over his shoulder as he rushed out of the room. "I've got an idea."

When he returned, Simon was clutching both halves of the electronic baby monitor his parents used to listen in on the twins when they were in another room.

Ruthie watched her brother with curiosity.

"Come on, Happy!" Simon called, patting his legs. The dog rushed to his side, tail wagging.

While Ruthie watched, Simon placed half the monitor in Happy's collar, hiding it under the dog's thick fur and floppy ears.

Not satisfied, Simon grabbed a bandanna and tied it around Happy's collar.

"Now go, Happy!" Simon commanded. "Go see Mary!"

Happy barked and sat down.

"Go!" Simon insisted. "Go see Mary. You know. *Mary.* Now go!"

Happy ran out of the room, her long claws tapping on the hardwood floor.

"I hope she goes to the right place this time," Ruthie said.

"I know," Simon agreed. "It took a big hunk out of my savings the last time I tried this, when Happy went under the Tripps' sprinkler system."

Ruthie peeked out the window. "Not to worry. The Tripps aren't watering their lawn."

Then Simon activated the monitor and they began to listen.

Reverend Camden leaned back in his office chair and put his chin on his hands. The door to his home office was ajar; the rest of the house was quiet.

Too quiet, Reverend Camden thought warily.

"Knock, knock," Lucy said as she pushed the door open.

"Hey," Reverend Camden said. "Come on in."

Lucy sat down.

"So how did it go in your student court today?" he asked.

"We didn't have it because of the big team meeting."

"I have something for you," said Reverend Camden as he put a heavy book down on his desk and tapped the title. *"Religion and the Law,"* he read aloud. "We have so much in common, there's a book about it."

Lucy broke into a grin. "Wow! Thank you."

"There's some interesting stuff in there," her father continued. "And coming from our similar positions, there's probably a lot we can talk about. You know, if you feel like it."

Lucy stopped flipping through the pages and her smile widened. "That would be great!"

Reverend Camden sat back and put his arms behind his head. At least there was *one* daughter he didn't have to worry about.

Happy pressed her nose against Mary's

door, pushed it open, and trotted in.

Mary was on the telephone, talking intently. She didn't even look up when the dog settled at her feet.

"I can't believe any of this is happening, Corey," Mary said. "My own parents stabbed me in the back."

Happy yawned and rolled over. Under the bandanna, the baby monitor did its job.

"I don't know," Mary continued. "What do you have in mind?"

Her eyes widened as she listened to Corey's plan. "That last part is a little extreme," she said. "But I can handle the part where we get something to eat."

"Extreme?" Ruthie said, listening from one floor below. *"What's* extreme?"

"Mary's exact words were 'That last part is a *little extreme,*'" Simon said. "I'm not sure what that means, but it definitely means *something*."

Ruthie scratched her head. "Should we tell Mom and Dad?"

"Probably."

Just then, Matt called from downstairs. "Let's go, Simon! We have to pick up the pizza before the game starts."

"Oh, boy!" Simon cried. "Guys' night out!"

He jumped up and headed for the staircase. Ruthie followed, too.

By the time they reached the front door, Mary's ominous words had been quickly forgotten.

"Don't worry, Dad," Simon said to his father, who was standing by Matt in the foyer. "I'll put some money in the pot for you."

He looked up to his older brother. "That's what we guys do, right, Matt? Eat pizza, make bets on the game, try to cover the spread."

Matt shrugged. "I guess."

Simon threw on his jacket as Matt opened the front door. Ruthie grabbed her jacket, too.

"You can't go!" Simon said. "You're no guy."

Ruthie crossed her arms and made a face. "I'm just as good a guy as any of you."

"Ruthie," Mrs. Camden called from the living room. "Why don't you stay home and do something with Lucy and me?"

"Kill me," Ruthie said, rolling her eyes. "No, thank you very much. I would much rather go to guys' night at Matt's."

Matt shrugged again. "It's okay with me if it's okay with you two," he told his parents.

Mrs. Camden stepped into the foyer. "How 'guy' is the evening going to be?" she asked.

"Typical stuff," Matt replied. "No big deal."

"You know," Ruthie said. "I *do* go to school, I play on a football team, and I've seen MTV. So, if there's something else out there, I say bring it on."

"That's so reassuring, my little flower," Reverend Camden quipped.

Ruthie shrugged and followed her brothers out to Matt's Camaro.

"Well, they're off," said Reverend Camden, closing the front door behind them. "Let's go upstairs."

When they reached the second floor hallway, they saw Mary approaching them. Her jacket was on.

"Hey, Mom. Hey, Dad," Mary said. "Since it's not a school night, would it be *okay* if I went out to eat with some girls from the team?" she said, her tone dripping with sarcasm. "Or am I *grounded* because of everything that's been going on?"

It was obvious that Mary was still angry with them. Her expression was smug, her tone snide.

"I know that you're upset," Mrs. Camden said tightly. "But I'd appreciate it if you'd watch your tone."

"I'm sorry." This time Mary's voice was more controlled, but it was clear she was still angry.

The doorbell rang. Mary's parents looked at her warily.

"My friends. They were just going to drop by to see if I could go with them," Mary said. "But I'll just tell them that I can't."

"We understand that you might want to vent with your friends," Reverend Camden said. "So, just do it quickly and then come right home."

"Thank you," Mary said, then turned away.

Mrs. Camden watched Mary go. "I hope we did the right thing."

"She can blow off some steam with her friends, and then we'll talk to her some more when she gets home," Reverend Camden said hopefully.

The usual Friday night crowd was hanging

out at the pool hall when the Lady Wildcats entered. But the room fell strangely quiet when Mary's group made their way to a table.

The girls ordered food and immediately began talking about the day's events.

"This whole thing stinks," Maggie said.

"The guys' team sure doesn't have to put up with this," Corey said. "In fact, no other team in the league has to put up with this."

"I don't appreciate being used as an example. Especially during my senior year," Mary added.

Maggie was so mad she couldn't sit still. She kept picking up her food and dropping it again. "This is my last year of high school basketball, too," she said. "I've worked since sixth grade to be on this team and the coach decides to go on a major power trip now?"

"No kidding," Elaine said with a nod. "Coach Cleary's a case."

Mary sighed. "Well, at least your dad didn't speak up and humiliate you in front of the world before stabbing you in the back."

"Well, they had help!" Karen shot back. "Did you hear Ms. Russell and Mr. Kent?"

"Something's got to be done," Maggie announced, her tone vengeful. The other girls nodded in agreement, including Mary.

Mrs. Camden was feeding Samuel while Reverend Camden placed David in his crib.

"Matt hasn't said anything more about moving back home since he said he was thinking about it," Reverend Camden said.

"I have a feeling it's going to come up again, don't you?" Mrs. Camden chuckled.

"Yeah," he nodded. "But we don't have to decide to do anything until he does."

They heard the front door open and two pairs of feet running up the stairs. Ruthie and Simon entered, with Matt on their heels.

"The game's over already?" Mrs. Camden asked, surprised.

"No," Simon said. "Ruthie's honking got to everyone and we were asked to leave."

Ruthie shrugged. "I was just being one of the guys."

"Honking doesn't make you a guy," Simon declared. "It makes you a pig."

Ruthie's jaw dropped.

"A pig who gets us kicked out of guys' night," Simon concluded.

"Okay, okay," Ruthie cried. "I'm not married to it. I thought that's what guys were supposed to do when they hung out."

"You were wrong," Simon said. "Very, very *toxically* wrong."

The reverend loudly cleared his throat and shot Simon a meaningful stare.

Simon sighed as he realized he'd just incriminated *himself* with his own words.

"Great!" he announced. "I just taught myself a lesson. I hope you're happy, Ruthie."

"Well," Ruthie replied, "I wouldn't say happy, exactly."

Mrs. Camden grabbed Ruthie's shoulders.

"You *know* how we feel about burping, sneezing on each other or each other's food, spitting, or anything to do with yours or anyone else's nose, and, yes, honking."

Ruthie nodded, and, from memory, recited the family mantra: "It's rude and gross, but accidents happen and you have to say excuse me. But accidents shouldn't happen *often*."

Mrs. Camden nodded. "Close enough."

Ruthie turned to Matt. "Excuse me," she said.

"You're *not* excused," Matt said. "But I forgive you."

"I'll take what I can get," Ruthie said, annoyed, and then she stomped out of the room.

"Is it okay if I finish watching the game downstairs?" Matt asked.

"Sure, son," Reverend Camden replied.

"Oh, yeah, I forgot," Ruthie said. "Could somebody please, please *finally* just tell me what this means?"

Before her stunned parents could stop her, Ruthie raised her hands and stuck out her middle fingers.

Less than an hour later, Reverend and Mrs. Camden were ready for bed. The twins were asleep, and Mrs. Camden had tucked Ruthie in for the night, after giving the girl a stern lecture on the proper use of her middle fingers. She noticed that her husband was lost in his own thoughts.

She poked him gently. "What's wrong?"

He shook his head and sighed. "I don't know. Lucy is doing great, but Mary...If I'd been on top of things and at my post, I might have seen this coming. Seen that her studies were slipping."

"Listen," Mrs. Camden said, poking him. "We love our kids, and we work really hard to be good parents who set the right kind of examples. But there comes a point in life when you just have to throw them out in the world and pray."

Reverend Camden frowned. "What about Mary?"

Mrs. Camden sighed. "Well," she said softly. "Maybe we threw her too far."

Then they both smiled.

"She's a good kid. We'll get through this," Mrs. Camden said, desperately trying to believe her own words.

Mary's palms were sweating as she followed her teammates up the walkway to the school's side entrance. She knew this was wrong, but she didn't care. She was too full of rage and hurt to care.

"I told you this would work," Maggie hissed as she jimmied open the door lock with her credit card. "I've used this door to sneak into school after I cut class lots of times."

"You cut class?" Corey said in mock seriousness.

The girls began to giggle, until Elaine shushed them. "Quiet!" she begged. "You don't want to get caught, do you?"

"There's nobody here," Karen insisted. "The school is dark."

Maggie pushed the door open and listened. The halls were silent. After a moment, she slipped into the darkened corridor.

"Let's go," she said, leading them inside. The only sound was the crackle of the brown paper bags they were carrying.

The other girls followed Maggie into the high school, Mary bringing up the rear. Her heart was racing as they stumbled through the pitch-black hallway.

Soon their eyes became accustomed to the dark, and they could find their way around. Maggie led the group toward the gym.

"Civil disobedience can be fun," Corey announced.

"Civil disobedience?" Karen said, giggling. "And I thought this was breaking and entering!"

"Yeah, well call it what you want," Maggie replied with a malicious grin. "We're already felons, and we haven't even started yet."

"Catch!" Karen hissed, tossing a can of spray paint to Maggie, then one to Elaine.

Elaine snapped hers out of the air, and presented it to the others.

"Good choice!" she whooped. "The school colors."

Then Karen thrust a paper bag into Mary's arms. "Let's see you shoot a few baskets with *those*."

Mary hefted a roll of toilet paper, aimed, and tossed. It arched gracefully across the court, between the steel ceiling beams, a long, white tail streaming behind.

To everyone's surprise, it dropped right through the hoop.

"Go, Camden!"

Mary whooped as she raced across the court and snatched up the paper roll again. This time she leaped, dunked it, and grabbed the net on the way down.

Mary hung suspended for a moment, until the fabric ripped and she dropped to the hardwood.

She looked up. Her teammates were busy, too.

Karen and Maggie were playing hockey with baseball bats and a plastic garbage can. With every blow, papers and trash scattered around the gym and the can bounced madly, like a rubber ball.

Elaine was busy painting the Wildcats

logo on the bleachers, the steel doors, and the walls.

The excitement was electric. Contagious. Mary laughed out loud, every nerve tingling. She'd felt this way a hundred times, in this very gym.

Alive. Powerful. In control.

Mary was finally taking back a vital part of her life. And it felt good.

Suddenly, a loud clang of metal doors snapped her back to reality. Mary was frozen in a beam of bright light.

She blinked, blinded.

"Stop!" a voice boomed from behind the brilliance. "You're all under arrest!"

TEN

The heavy steel door squeaked as it opened. Its metal bars gleamed dully in the dim light.

The uniformed policeman fumbled at his belt until he found the right key. With a sharp click, a second barred door was unlocked.

"This way," Sergeant Michaels said, his voice echoing hollowly off the concrete walls.

With hands joined for mutual support, Reverend and Mrs. Camden anxiously followed their old friend through the depths of the town jail.

Ahead, in the dimness, they could hear urgent whispers. Someone—a man—cried out in the throes of a nightmare. His cry rebounded off the walls and faded.

"Right here," the policeman said, placing another key in a lock.

The cell door opened, and Mrs. Camden gasped.

Mary looked up at her parents, her face pale. She looked small and frail in the dingy jail cell, and despite the anger and shock she felt, Mrs. Camden wanted nothing so much as to take her daughter in her arms and shield her from the world.

But Mrs. Camden knew it was far too late for that.

"Thank you," Reverend Camden said hoarsely to the policeman. Sergeant Michaels nodded, but didn't smile.

"If you need any help," he said. "Finding a lawyer..."

"What?" Mrs. Camden's head jerked at those words.

Sergeant Michaels cleared his throat. "We're releasing her without bail," he explained. "But this isn't over. She's—"

Sergeant Michaels halted. When he spoke again, his voice was gentle. "You're going to need a lawyer," he stated again.

Reverend Camden nodded. Mrs. Camden fought off tears. Mary looked down at her feet, refusing to meet her parents' gaze.

"Yeah, okay," Reverend Camden said. "Thank you, Ben."

The policeman nodded. Reverend Camden took his daughter's arm and led her out of the jail cell.

Back at the Camden household, Matt was nervously pacing the living room, Ruthie trailing his every step.

For the tenth time in the past twenty minutes, he stopped, pulled the curtains aside, and peered into the darkness.

"Come away," Lucy said, throwing a pillow at Matt's back. "Waiting at the window isn't going to get Mom, Dad, and Mary home any faster."

Matt picked up the pillow and threw it back at Lucy as Simon entered the living room with four big bags of snack food.

When he reached Lucy, she and Matt descended on him. Bags ripped simultaneously and everyone began to loudly crunch.

"There's no reason to be nervous," Matt insisted, stuffing his face with cheese curls. "Mom and Dad said Mary was fine."

"No," Lucy corrected him, around a mouthful of potato chips. "They said that

Mary *wasn't hurt,* which isn't the same thing as *fine."*

"So?"

"So, let me tell you something I picked up from student court," Lucy said, wiping the crumbs from her mouth. "When people start choosing their words *too* carefully, it's not good."

"Yeah. Like those lawyers in Washington," quipped Simon, punctuating his joke with the crunch of a corn chip.

"Chill," Matt warned. "Let's not get all freaked out until we know something. I mean, right now, we don't know *anything.* Maybe somebody had car trouble, or—"

"No way!" Simon cried, cutting him off. "That place between Dad's eyebrows was all knotted up, and he wasn't squinting."

"And Mom wasn't wearing lipstick," Ruthie added. "Mom always puts on lipstick when she leaves the house, even when she goes to Home Depot."

Simon pondered his sister's words.

"Mom was wearing lipstick that time Mary got detention," he said. "And the time she shoved that guy's head into the toilet. Even the time she wrecked the car with you."

"No lipstick is no good," Ruthie stated firmly.

"I hate to say it," Lucy sighed. "But this time, Ruthie's right."

Ruthie smiled smugly. "Well, you better get used to saying it," she announced. "Because I'm older now. I'm in the game."

"What game?" Lucy asked.

"The game of life."

Lucy glanced at Matt, then at Simon.

She might be right, Lucy decided.

But Ruthie ruined the effect by burping loudly.

"Excuse me," she said quickly. "I wasn't trying to be a guy this time. It *was* an accident."

Ruthie rubbed her tummy. "When I'm nervous, my stomach goes crazy and I burp."

Simon nodded, dropping the bag of chips. "Me, too."

Matt took the bag of potato chips. "Why don't you all go to bed," he said. "I'll wait up for Mom and Dad and tell you about it in the morning."

Everyone burst out laughing.

"No way I'm missing this," Lucy said.

Just then, a car pulled into the driveway.

Everyone stopped laughing and got very quiet.

"Plan B!" Simon cried.

Instantly, Lucy, Simon, and even Ruthie pretended to be fast asleep, as if they were watching television when they'd passed out.

Matt stared at his siblings with disgust as the front door opened. *Like anyone would fall for that!*

Grim-faced, Reverend Camden came into the living room, followed by his wife.

Mary entered the house behind them, but rushed up the stairs without saying a word to anyone.

Mrs. Camden rolled her eyes when she saw the kids in the living room.

"It's late," Reverend Camden said, shaking Lucy, then Simon. "Go to bed. We'll talk about what happened in the morning."

Mrs. Camden plopped down on the couch after the others headed upstairs.

"What are we going to do?" she said anxiously.

Reverend Camden sighed as he sat down next to her. "Call around and get a lawyer, I guess."

Mrs. Camden took her husband's hand. He kissed her.

"Didn't see this one coming," he said after a pause.

"Not this," Mrs. Camden replied sadly, shaking her head. "Not in a million years."

They sat together in silence, holding hands in the darkened living room until far into the early morning hours.

Lucy found her sister lying on her bed in the dark. She was hugging her pillow and fighting back tears.

"Mary? What—"

"We trashed the school gym," Mary said softly. She did not meet Lucy's gaze.

"Who? Who trashed the gym?"

Mary shrugged. "Some girls from the team and me," she answered.

Lucy dropped onto the bed, hardly able to believe it. "Why?" she demanded.

"I don't know," Mary said, finally looking up. "We were eating and talking about the team lockout, and it just happened."

Lucy shook her head. "Nothing just happens."

"Whatever…" Mary said sadly, hugging the pillow even tighter.

"So…you got busted?" Lucy felt numbed by the news.

Mary nodded. "We must have set off a

silent alarm or something, because the police showed up pretty fast."

"What's going to happen?" Lucy asked softly.

"I don't know," Mary said, her voice breaking. "But Sergeant Michaels said I need a lawyer."

Lucy stared at her sister, dumb-founded. "This is unreal."

"I wish," Mary said, wiping her wet cheeks.

Simon was almost asleep when Happy crawled onto the bed beside him. He reached out and stroked the dog's fur. His fingers closed on the bandanna around Happy's collar, and the baby monitor still hidden beneath it.

Simon opened his eyes and sat up in the bed.

On his desk, he could see the other half of the baby monitor—the part through which he and Ruthie had listened to Mary's conversation earlier that evening.

Over and over again, Mary's words ran through Simon's head: *"That part is a little extreme."*

He pulled the covers off and grabbed both halves of the baby monitor. Simon went to the door and checked the hall before he scurried to Ruthie's room.

"Do you know what this means?" Simon said as he rushed into his little sister's room. Ruthie put down the binoculars and looked at the baby monitor in Simon's hand.

"Those babies are still here?" Ruthie offered.

"Those babies are our *brothers* and they have names," Simon said. "And they're not going anywhere."

Ruthie shrugged.

"Things change," she announced. "Hospitals make mistakes. Any day now their real parents from Canada could show up and want them back. It'll be hard for Mom and Dad, but they'll do the right thing. That's why I'm not getting attached to those *babies*."

Ruthie patted her chest.

"Heartbreak is a terrible thing."

"Keep telling yourself tales," Simon replied. "You're just jealous because those babies—"

Simon caught himself. "—Our *brothers* took over your spot as the family baby."

"You don't know me at all, Simon."

Ruthie put the binoculars back to her

eyes and peered through the window. Simon crossed the room and put the baby monitor on the windowsill. Ruthie blinked and looked at it.

"Remember?" Simon prompted. "We were listening to Mary on the phone? She said something about the 'last part being extreme'? And we didn't know what it meant but we knew it meant something and we were going to tell Mom and Dad, but—"

"We forgot!" Ruthie interrupted.

"Because we went to guys' night at Matt's," Simon concluded.

They exchanged meaningful glances.

"I'll bet that whatever the extreme thing was, Mary did it tonight, and that's why she's in major trouble, and Mom and Dad are so upset," Simon said.

"If we had warned them, this might not have happened," Ruthie added.

"But we didn't."

Ruthie dropped the binoculars on her bed.

"That's it, then. It's over," she declared, throwing her arms wide. "We're going to Hell."

Simon stared at his sister.

"Don't give me that look," Ruthie cried.

"I didn't mean it like a bad word, I meant it like the place."

"I know," Simon said with shaking head. "I gave you that look because you might just be right."

Ruthie burped and rubbed her tummy. Then it was Simon's turn to burp.

"Excuse me," Ruthie said. "Nervous tummy."

"Yeah," Simon replied. "Mine, too."

ELEVEN

Reverend Camden got up early the next morning. He quietly slipped on some clothes and went out to the minivan.

Traffic was light as he drove to the high school. When he got there, he noticed a police car parked near the school entrance and a Channel Eight news van sitting across the street.

Apparently, news traveled fast.

Reverend Camden parked the family van and ducked into the school as fast as he could. The halls were empty as he made his way through them. He stopped dead when he saw the yellow police tape blocking the entrance to the gym.

Somehow that simple string of yellow

ribbon brought last night's events into sharp focus.

"Are you looking for the principal?"

Reverend Camden turned to find Mr. Kent, the athletic director. He was flanked by two policemen, one in uniform, one in a plain dark suit. The plainclothed cop had a sour look on his face.

"Hello, Mr. Kent," the reverend replied. "Yes, I *am* looking for the principal."

"She's inside the gym," Mr. Kent said with a frown. "With the insurance adjuster."

"I'd like to see her, if possible," Reverend Camden said as he moved toward the door.

"That's a crime scene, sir," the uniformed officer said. "You can't—"

"Let him go," the plainclothed officer interrupted. "The perps were caught red-handed."

Then the plainclothed policeman locked eyes with Reverend Camden. "This case is closed," the detective said.

Reverend Camden nodded sadly and ducked under the yellow tape. When he finally entered the gymnasium, he was not prepared for what he found.

When he'd first heard about the incident, Reverend Camden had thought the girls had thrown some toilet paper over the bleachers and maybe scattered some wastepaper around—certainly nothing that would have done major damage.

Well, there was plenty of toilet paper, all right. And paper *was* strewn all over the gym—but there was much more than he'd ever imagined. So much more...

Trash cans had been overturned and the sloppy wet contents strewn all over the floor. Crushed soda cans, plastic wrappers, banana peels—anything a high school kid would throw into a trash bin was now littering the gym floor. And there were long trails of spray paint. Lots of them. Garish splotches covered the walls, the bleachers, the fire doors, even the windows. The hoops were torn down, the backboards stained. And empty paint cans still lay where they were dropped.

On the other side of the room, Principal Russell stood with a grim-faced man, the insurance adjuster. The man clutched a camera, which he flashed repeatedly.

Reverend Camden walked around and took a closer look at the damage.

How much more damage would they

have done if the police hadn't caught them? he wondered.

His shock was obvious to Principal Russell from across the room.

"Excuse me a minute," she said to the insurance adjuster. The man nodded and continued to snap pictures of the damage.

"Hello, Reverend," Principal Russell said.

He turned and opened his mouth to speak. But no words would come. Finally, he found his voice.

"I'm...so sorry," he said, his voice breaking.

Ms. Russell nodded. "Me, too."

They stood silently for a moment, then the principal spoke.

"Thanks for your support," she said softly. "At the meeting yesterday, I mean. Most of the other parents didn't see it the way you and I did."

The woman sighed. "I just wish that more people—more students—saw things our way. The educational system would be a better place."

Reverend Camden shook his head. "I just wish that it all hadn't led to this."

"You two could help out, you know," Mrs.

Camden said as she went by, a twin in each arm.

"Where's Dad?" Ruthie asked.

"He had to go out," Mrs. Camden replied tensely. When she looked away, Simon poked Ruthie and put his finger to his lips.

Ruthie winked and zipped her lips.

"What do you want us to do, Mom?" Simon asked.

"Pick up the baby toys in the twins' room," she said over her shoulder. "Then clean up your own rooms."

When she was gone, Simon looked at Ruthie.

"Did Mary look different to you this morning?"

Ruthie thought about it. "Different how?"

"I don't know," Simon shrugged. "More dangerous? More like a bad guy?"

Ruthie scrunched up her face, then nodded.

"Mom and Dad didn't look so good, either," Simon said as he led his sister into the twins' room.

"I know," Ruthie replied as she began to pick up baby toys. "It scares me when they look like that."

Simon threw a bunch of squeeze toys into the playpen, sure they'd just be thrown out again when the twins returned.

"None of this would have happened if I had just remembered to tell Mom and Dad what we heard last night," Simon said, frowning. "This whole thing is my fault."

Ruthie nodded again. Simon shot her an evil look.

"But I helped it be your fault," Ruthie added hastily.

Simon bent over to pick up a stuffed bear. Then he rubbed his tummy.

"Does your stomach feel like it's kind of sick?" he asked.

Ruthie burped. "Excuse me," she said immediately.

"It's guilt gut."

Ruthie scratched her head. "What's that?"

"It's when you feel so bad about something your stomach hurts."

Ruthie nodded as the realization came to her. "Then I've got guilt gut, all right!"

She threw an armful of toys into the playpen. "Should we tell Mom and Dad?"

"No," Simon said. "They have enough to worry about."

Ruthie rubbed her tummy and frowned.

"Anyway," Simon continued. "Dad's heart is under enough stress right now. If he found out this whole thing could have been avoided, it'd probably explode."

Ruthie blinked in horror.

"And if Dad had more heart trouble, it would just mean more guilt for us," Simon concluded.

"Will we never be free?" Ruthie cried.

Simon sat down on a chair and hung his head. "I don't know."

"Well, that's just not good enough!" Ruthie declared. "We have to do something. I don't want to have guilt gut and go to...well, you know where."

"Yes, I do," Simon replied. "And I don't want to go there either."

Simon thought about it for a moment. Then he slapped his knee.

"I've got it!" he cried, jumping to his feet. "God's the answer!"

"Huh?"

"He helped us get Happy, and twin brothers, too," Simon explained. "And God made sure Dad was okay after his heart attack."

"Well, let's give Him a whirl." Ruthie shrugged. "What do we have to lose?"

Simon burped. "Nothing but guilt gut," he said.

Mrs. Camden sat down on the couch and turned on the television. The Channel Eight noon news was covering the school vandalism.

She switched the TV off again. Mrs. Camden realized she was beginning to hate Carrie Chadwick's face.

The front door opened and Reverend Camden came in, carrying an armload of dry cleaning swathed in plastic bags.

"Did Bill Mays return my call?" he asked as he hung up the clothes.

"He did better than that," Mrs. Camden announced. "He said he'd be right over to see what he could do."

Reverend Camden breathed a sigh of relief. "A lawyer who makes house calls. Unbelievable."

"Well," Mrs. Camden added, "you baptized all of his children, helped two of them get summer jobs, and talked one of them out of an ill-advised body piercing. I guess he felt it was the least he could do."

The doorbell rang, and Reverend

Camden hurried into the foyer.

"Hi, Bill! I can't thank you enough for coming over," Reverend Camden said as the balding, middle-aged man entered the house.

"No problem, Reverend," the man said jovially. Then, "Hello, Annie. Sorry this couldn't be a social call."

"Me, too, Bill," she replied. "How's Martha?"

Mrs. Camden showed the lawyer into the living room while Reverend Camden rushed upstairs to fetch Mary. When she came down, everyone in the room rose to greet her.

"Mary," Mrs. Camden said, rising. "You remember Mr. Mays from church?"

Mary nodded guardedly. "Uh...hi, Mr. Mays."

"Hello, Mary," the lawyer said, watching the girl intently.

"Bill is going to help us out with...everything," Reverend Camden said tactfully.

But Bill Mays cleared his throat. "He's going to *try*," he said. Then the lawyer looked hard at Mary's parents.

"I spoke with Ms. Russell, the school principal—"

"So did I," Reverend Camden interjected.

"She said that you and the other students who...caused the incident will have to appear in student court."

Mary shook her head, her eyes downcast.

"Of course," the lawyer added, "the worst that can happen there is a simple expulsion."

Mary was surprised. "Expulsion?"

"Sorry," Bill Mays continued. "But that's just the school side of it. I haven't spoken with the prosecutor's office yet, but after reading Sergeant Michaels's report, I'm pretty sure that Mary will be charged with wanton destruction of property and vandalism."

Reverend Camden and his wife exchanged pained glances.

"That means a fine of fifteen hundred dollars," the lawyer explained. "Or three times the value of the damage, whichever is more."

Mary winced. *How will I ever come up with that kind of money?* she wondered.

"It also means no more than two and a half years in prison, and no less than two and a half months."

The Camdens were speechless. The room was so quiet that Bill Mays could hear the clock ticking on the mantel.

Finally, Mrs. Camden leaned forward and spoke.

"Maybe you've forgotten, Bill," she said. "Mary is only seventeen. She's still a minor."

But the lawyer shook his head.

"At seventeen, she is almost an adult, and she's certainly not going to be viewed as a minor child in the eyes of the court."

Mrs. Camden paled and sat back again.

"But there is another course of action, and I'm going to pursue it on your behalf," Bill Mays explained.

"What's that?" Reverend Camden asked hopefully.

"It's called the Diversion Program," the lawyer said. "The program was designed as a way to divert some people from the criminal justice system before it's too late."

Mrs. Camden frowned.

She didn't like the idea of Mary being a potential criminal. Then, she realized that, in the eyes of the law, Mary already was a criminal—or would be after sentencing.

"The Diversion Program involves probation, community service, weekly counseling sessions, classes on victim impact, or whatever else the probation officer wants to tack on."

"That doesn't sound too bad," Reverend Camden said with false optimism.

"It's a one-time shot," Bill Mays warned them. Then he looked hard at Mary.

"And if you get in any more trouble in the future, the program will not be an option."

Mary took in the man's words. Then she nodded.

"If you successfully complete the program," the man concluded, "then your conviction will eventually be erased. It will be like it never happened."

But it did, Mary thought bitterly.

"So how do we get into this Diversion Program?" Mrs. Camden asked.

Bill Mays sat back in his chair.

"I've already set things in motion," he replied. "On Monday, I'll meet with the prosecutor and see if I can get the judge to hold off on setting a trial date while I walk Mary's application through the Diversion Program's red tape."

Reverend Camden studied the man's face. "But there are no guarantees, right? If Mary doesn't get into the program..." His voice trailed off, but the lawyer caught his meaning.

"Then there is a very real chance that Mary could go to jail," Bill Mays told them.

TWELVE

From the bench on the Camdens' front porch, Lucy watched the arrival of Bill Mays.

This whole situation is totally unbelievable, Lucy thought. *It's like I've suddenly been transported and now I'm part of some other family or something.*

Lucy sighed.

The only time I thought Mary would need a lawyer was when she was ready to sign her first multi-million-dollar athletic contract. Now her athletic career may be over for good.

"Hey, Lucy!"

Lucy looked up to find Rod Dietle and Shelby Corman waving to her.

"So," Rod said when they were

together on the porch, "how's Mary holding up?"

"They're talking to a lawyer right now."

Rod and Shelby exchanged surprised looks.

"The gym's off-limits to students," Shelby said. "But I guess the damage must have been pretty bad for Mary to need a lawyer."

Lucy nodded. "Mary will have to go before the student court, too."

"Compared to real court, how bad can it be?" Shelby asked.

"I've see people get expelled for less than what Mary and her friends did," Lucy said.

"You're *cold*, Lucy!" Rod cried with a shiver.

"Huh?"

"You'd throw your own sister out of school?"

"It's not up to me," Lucy returned.

"Maybe not," Rod said. "But as a member of the court, you'd be a part of the decision."

"I know," Lucy whispered.

"Don't worry," Shelby said. "Everybody's toilet-papered something *once* in their life. How bad could it be?"

"Yeah," Rod added. "It can't be *that* bad."

Lucy said nothing. *I should check out the damages myself,* she suddenly decided.

By the grins on their faces, Lucy knew that Rod and Shelby had both come up with the same idea.

It was dark in the narrow confessional. Simon pushed at Ruthie in the tiny space, but she pushed right back.

"How does anybody talk to God in here?" Ruthie wondered. "We have closets bigger than this."

The panel in front of them slid open. Through the thin screen, Simon and Ruthie could see the face of Father Hartman, the Catholic priest in charge of Saint Vincent's.

"Uh...hi," Simon began. "We're sorry to bother you, but we did something wrong and we thought if we talked to God and made it up to Him, He might make us feel better."

"Yeah," Ruthie added. "And we don't want to go, well, you know where. It's hot there! Not summer vacation hot, but *too* hot. If you know what I mean!"

"Yes." The priest nodded. "I think I do.

And I hear that a lot. So what happened?"

Simon took a deep breath. "In a nut-shell," he began. "We eavesdropped on our older sister because she was in a superbad mood—"

"Although sometimes we do it 'cause we're bored," Ruthie added. "Or even, to tell the truth, because we *like* to. Her life is very interesting."

Simon nudged Ruthie, and she stopped talking.

"Anyway," Simon said. "Her friends said something, we don't know what, because we were eavesdropping with a baby monitor, it wasn't like we had a wire-tap—"

"I wish!" Ruthie cried.

Simon frowned at her.

"Well, I *do!*" she insisted.

"We heard Mary—I mean, our *sister*, say something that didn't make any sense to us, but it meant something."

"Something bad," Ruthie added.

"Oh, yes." The priest smiled. "You're preaching to the choir now."

"So, we were going to tell our mom and dad, but we forgot," Simon went on. "And our sister did something bad, and it might not have happened if we had just remembered to tell them."

The priest thought about this for a moment.

"Oh, yeah," Simon added hastily. "I also gave the finger, but I already got in trouble and apologized for that."

"Me, too," Ruthie said. "But I was trying to get someone to tell me what it meant. Now I know...yikes!"

Father Hartman chuckled. "You're not Catholics, are you?"

"No. But is it okay that we're here?" Simon asked in a wary voice.

"Of course!"

"Oh, goodie," Ruthie said. "Because we have bad enough guilt gut already."

"I'm sorry to hear that," Father Hartman said in a voice that was filled with sympathy. "But the way I see it is that you've already confessed your sins, and seem truly sorry for them. And anyone who asks for God's forgiveness shall have it."

"You're kidding?" Simon said. "Just like that?"

Father Hartman shook his head sadly. "There *is* one more thing."

"I knew it!" Ruthie cried. "This whole thing was way too easy."

"You should perform an act of contrition," the priest continued.

"Okay," Simon said instantly. "Er... what is that?"

"It's a task," Father Hartman explained. "A good work that will help get you back on the right track."

Simon thought about it. "That's exactly what we're looking for."

"One of the Ten Commandments is *Honor thy father and mother.* So, you must honor them by being truthful and up front about everything you told me. You will feel much better if you do."

Then Father Hartman offered them his blessing.

"Thank you," they said as one.

Simon and Ruthie exited the confessional stiff and sweaty.

"They should make those rooms bigger," Ruthie complained. "You almost poked my eye out with your pointy hair."

"I don't think it was designed for two."

"I've heard that confession is good for the soul," Ruthie announced. "And I have to say it gets my thumbs-up."

"Well," Simon complained. "Confession or not, my guilt gut is *still* killing me."

*   *   *

Lucy, Rod, and Shelby quick-walked the two and a half miles to Glenoak's Kennedy High School in record time. Lucy was hot and sweaty when they arrived, despite the coolness of the day.

"Now, how do we get in?" Lucy asked. "The whole place looks deserted."

She turned to Rod Dietle. "I thought you had a plan."

"You forget," Rod said smugly. "I'm in charge of audiovisuals!"

"So what?" Shelby said.

"So," Rod replied as he fumbled in his jacket, "I have a key!" He produced a key ring with what looked to be a hundred keys on it.

"It's a wonder you don't set off a metal detector," said Shelby.

"Sometimes I do."

"Hurry up," Lucy cried, shivering.

Rod stuck the key in the lock and turned it. Shelby and Lucy rushed through the door behind him.

"Let's go!" Shelby said.

"Wait a minute!" Rod cried. "Do you want to get arrested for breaking and entering?"

Rod went over to a metal box on the wall near the front doors. It had a bunch of numbered keys and a blinking red light on it. He placed a smaller key in the box lock and turned it. Then he punched a bunch of numbers. The blinking red light turned to a steady green.

"Now the silent alarm has been deactivated," Rod explained.

Lucy shivered again. But this time it wasn't the cold. "A silent alarm," she whispered. "I guess that's how they caught Mary."

"Let's go," Rod said, leading them through the deserted hallways.

The double doors that led to the gym were crisscrossed with yellow police ribbon. Rod and Shelby stuck their heads between the strands and peered inside.

"Okay," Rod said, shaking his head in amazement. "I *never* did anything like this."

"Wow," said Shelby, a look of profound shock on her face. "I did not imagine *this!*"

With mounting apprehension, Lucy peered into the gym. "Oh, God," she whispered. "I can't believe my own sister could do something like this."

Shelby put her hand on Lucy's shoulder. "Yeah," she said. "But she didn't do it alone. She had a lot of help."

But her words could not stem the tide of tears that ran down Lucy's cheeks. "I know," she said. "But still…"

"Yeah," Rod said, nodding. "This *is* bad."

Rod and Shelby could see that Lucy was taking things hard. Lucy leaned against them for support as they continued their unauthorized tour of the crime scene.

Matt was about to unlock the door to his apartment when it flew open. Matt and Shana were both startled when Mark Carlington, a guy Matt knew from history class, came through the door.

"Hey, Matt," Mark said. "I was just leaving."

He departed, and Matt ushered Shana into the apartment.

"Hey, Hamilton," Matt said when he saw his roommate. He pointed at the front door with his thumb. "What was he doing here?"

"He was interested in taking over your half of the rent," John said. "*If* you decide you *have* to move back home, that is."

Matt was surprised.

"I'm not trying to push you out," John

quickly explained. "But I've got to cover my bases and make sure my business is going to be taken care of. The same way you're taking care of *your* business with your family."

Matt nodded. "I understand."

John began to gather up his books and stuff them into his backpack. "Is your sister all right?" he asked.

"She's in major, get-a-lawyer trouble."

"I'm sorry," John said. "I guess that means that you're done thinking about moving out."

Matt nodded. The awkward moment stretched on.

"Well, then," John said with a frown. "It's been great. Tell your family hi, and I hope everything works out with Mary and all."

Matt wasn't sure what to say. "I guess I'll see you around," he finally managed.

John nodded, then turned and left. As he closed the front door, Shana began to search the cupboards for something to eat.

"It's probably for the best," Matt reasoned, rubbing the back of his neck. "Things have been a little strained around here lately."

Shana closed the refrigerator. "Well," she said. "You were the one who dropped the moving-home bomb on him, what, twenty-four hours ago?"

"It's not like I planned this stuff with my family," Matt said defensively.

"I know, I know." Shana hugged him.

"And part of the reason I think you're so great is because you love your family so much," she said. "But if you spent one fourth the time at the grocery store that you do at your parents' house, you might not be so frustrated. Or so hungry."

Matt snorted. "With everything that's going on with my family, *that's* what you say?"

"Truth hurts."

"What?"

"Look," Shana explained. "I get the stuff with your family, I really do. I love your family, too. But I know what you're going through. It's tough living on your own. I felt the same way when I moved out. I just didn't have your kind of family to fall back on."

"Meaning?"

"Meaning I *had* to make it on my own," Shana said. "I had no choice."

"You know, not having a family to lean

on also meant that you didn't have a family to worry about," Matt argued. "You really didn't have to worry about anyone except yourself."

Shana's eyes went wide. "That's not true!" she cried. "I worried about my mom and my brother, but there came a point when I realized that there was nothing I could do for them *except* worry, and that wasn't the same as being helpful or constructive."

"Yeah," Matt said. "But our situations are different."

"Yes, they are," Shana said, pulling him close. "And now I have *you* to worry about."

Matt faced her, his face tight.

"And I *do* care," Shana sighed. "A lot."

"I care about you, too," he whispered. "But right now, after this conversation, I don't feel like you know me at all."

Shana looked into Matt's eyes. She saw anger and hurt. Neither of them spoke for a long time.

Then Shana gathered up her stuff, put her jacket on, and left without even a goodbye.

THIRTEEN

The synagogue was empty when Simon and Ruthie arrived. Ruthie's eyes were drawn to the Torah in its beautiful case at the front of the room.

"Wow," she whispered. "How cool is that?"

"I'd have to say it's pretty cool."

The voice from behind made Simon and Ruthie jump.

"Did I frighten you?" Rabbi Cohen asked.

"Er, no," Simon stammered. "I thought we were alone."

"You're never alone here," Rabbi Cohen said.

"We're sorry to bother you. Is it okay if we're in here?" Simon asked.

Rabbi Cohen nodded. "Of course."

"Oh, good," Simon said. "Because we feel terrible enough already about everything else. Including giving the finger, but not as much as the whole thing with our sister—"

Simon was speaking so fast that his words were running together. Rabbi Cohen raised his hand to slow Simon down.

"Nutshell," the boy continued after a pause. "We forgot to tell our parents something we overheard our sister say that didn't make any sense to us, but it meant something."

"Not a good something," Ruthie added.

Simon nodded.

"And now we have guilt gut," Ruthie continued. "And we don't want to go to, well, you know where."

Rabbi Cohen scratched his head.

"You *know*," Ruthie coached. "To that place that is really hot. Hot tub hot, but it's not relaxing to your muscles?"

"Ah, yes," Rabbi Cohen said finally. "You're not Jewish, are you?"

Simon and Ruthie shook their heads.

"Well," the rabbi continued, "we don't believe in Hell."

Ruthie poked Simon's ribs. "I see a

loophole," she whispered excitedly.

When they were all seated, Rabbi Cohen tried to explain his beliefs to them.

"For us, God is like a giant pool filled with the brightest light you'll ever see," he began. "And we all come from that pool and have some of God's bright light in all of us."

Simon listened attentively. Ruthie did, too.

"Every time we sin," the rabbi continued, "our light gets a little dimmer. And eventually, at the end of our life, everyone goes back to God's pool."

"Sounds good," Simon said. "But we don't want to have the dimmest lights in the pool when we get back. Everyone would know that we're like major losers. How pathetic and embarrassing would that be?

"No," Simon sighed. "We have to get our lights bright again."

"Traditionally, Jewish people atone, or make up for their sins, once a year, during Yom Kippur," the rabbi explained. "I hate to be the one to tell you this, but you've already missed it for the year."

"But we can't wait a whole year to make up for this!" Simon cried.

"Our dim lights are giving us guilt gut," Ruthie moaned.

"I'm sorry," Rabbi Cohen said. "But you know you can't control other people's free will, even if you could see these things coming, which, most of the time, you can't."

Ruthie and Simon frowned.

"In the meantime," Rabbi Cohen said, "I think you should talk to your parents. You'll feel better."

Simon thanked the rabbi, and then took Ruthie's hand. Outside, Ruthie took a deep breath.

"I feel better already."

"You said that after we talked to Father Hartman," Simon said. "But your guilt gut came back again, anyway."

Across town, at Mary's high school, the janitor pushed the double doors open for Mrs. Camden.

"You were lucky to find me here," the man said. "Usually I'm not around on Saturdays, but because of…well, you know.

"The principal wants me to wax the hall floors today, because on Monday we're going to tackle the gym."

"Thank you," Mrs. Camden said. "I'll only be a minute. I still have to go pick up a couple of pizzas for the family's dinner."

The man nodded and stepped aside.

"Just be careful you don't break the police tape. I'll be out here if you need me."

Mrs. Camden nodded and the janitor returned to his work. For a long time, she waited at the threshold before she mustered up enough courage to step inside. Then Mrs. Camden took a deep breath and climbed between the yellow strands of tape.

What she saw inside the gym brought tears to her eyes.

"Oh, Mary, how could you?" she whispered. "How could you do this?"

Reverend Camden was heading for his office when Matt came through the front door. He was carrying a duffel bag over his shoulder and a gym bag in his hand.

"More laundry?" Reverend Camden quipped. "It can't be yours. Are you taking in other people's wash now?"

"Ha, ha," Matt said, not amused. "Not exactly."

"So what is going on?" his father asked.

"It's most of my stuff," Matt explained. "With everything that's been going on lately, I've decided I should move back home."

His father looked at him with a puzzled expression.

"To help out," Matt continued. "Sort of keep an eye on things."

"Oh," Reverend Camden said, blinking. "That's very...thoughtful. Thank you, son."

Matt broke into a grin. He slapped his father playfully on the back.

"Don't worry, Dad," he said. "I'll take care of all the arrangements myself."

"You know, son—"

Mary came rushing downstairs. Her face was pale and she looked as if she was about to cry. "I...I just got off the phone with Mr. Wolf," she said.

"Mr. Wolf?" her father said. "The man from the group that gave you the scholarship?"

"Apparently, word of what happened has gotten around," Mary continued, her voice shaky. "And in light of everything that's gone on, including my recent subpar academic performance, Mr. Wolf said that the scholarship committee felt that there were better candidates out there for the limited funds they have to donate."

Mary paused, her eyes welling with tears.

"I lost my scholarship," she told them.

FOURTEEN

Lucy found Mary in their bedroom. She was sprawled on her bed, a pillow over her face. Lucy cleared her throat, but Mary didn't stir.

"Mom'll be home soon with the pizza," Lucy informed her.

There was no reply.

Lucy took a deep breath, steeled herself, then crossed the room. In one quick motion, she ripped the pillow away from Mary's face.

"Dad told me what happened with your scholarship," Lucy said. "And I'm sorry. Everybody is."

"Yeah," Mary moaned, turning over on her tummy and hiding her face in her hands. "But *you* think I deserve it."

Lucy sat down on the bed. "I've never known you when you weren't playing basketball," she began. "You spent many years earning that scholarship. So, no, I don't think you deserve to have it all taken away."

Mary peeked out from between her fingers. "But...?"

"But," Lucy said, her tone harsher than she meant it to be. "I saw the gym."

"And you think I deserve jail time," Mary said. "Because that's a real possibility."

"Dad told me that, too." Lucy frowned. "I don't know what to say or think. Nothing like this has ever happened to anyone I know."

Mary looked away. When she spoke again, her voice was flat and unemotional. "Well, I'm in new territory myself."

Mary sat up in the bed and faced Lucy.

"What do you think should happen to me?" she demanded. "You're on the student court. You have to figure out what to do in these kinds of cases all the time."

"You're my *sister*, not a *case*."

Before Mary could reply, Matt appeared at the door with a duffel bag over one shoulder and a gym bag in his hand. He was smiling.

"Hey," he said. "I just wanted to let you know that I'm moving back home so—"

"Oh, no you don't, buster!" Lucy cried. "You are *not* getting this room back!"

Matt blinked in shock. He didn't expect defiance, especially not from Lucy.

"Come on!" Matt said. "I was here before either of you. And not just in this room. In this house, and in this *family*."

"As you know, I just lost my college scholarship, so I probably won't be going anywhere, ever again," Mary said, "except maybe to jail. But otherwise, I'll probably die of old age in this house. And I plan to do it in this *room*. So maybe you and Lucy can talk about being roomies when and if they haul me off to prison, okay?"

Matt was dumbfounded. He never expected to take flak from both his sisters.

"Okay, Matt," Lucy said after a long silence.

At last, he thought. *The voice of reason.*

Then Lucy shoved him into the hall. "Welcome home," she said before slamming the door in his face.

Lucy faced Mary again. "I don't want you to get expelled from school," she said. "But as for the rest of it, I don't have a clue."

Mary nodded and smiled weakly. Lucy departed. She closed the door behind her.

"Me neither," Mary whispered sadly.

Simon watched his brother as Matt unpacked his duffel bag and placed the stuff on the extra bed in his bedroom. Ruthie watched, too.

Simon rolled his eyes when Matt tossed the empty duffel in the corner of his tidy room.

"Exactly how long are you planning to visit?" Simon asked pointedly.

"I'm not visiting," Matt insisted. "I'm here to stay. I'm moving back home."

"Did you flunk out?" Ruthie asked.

"No, of course not!"

"Were you expelled, like Simon?"

"I was *suspended*," Simon protested.

"Nothing like that happened, Ruthie," Matt said.

"Then what happened to *independence*?" Simon cried. "What happened to the freedom of not having to put the toilet seat down if you don't want to? What happened to partying it up in your own pad?"

"Yeah," Ruthie added. "And what about *chicks*?"

Matt faced his siblings. "What happened is that Mom had two babies and Dad had a heart attack," he said. Then he pointed at Simon and Ruthie.

"And *you* got suspended for giving the finger. And you grossed out the world by trying to act like a guy." Matt shook his head.

"And as for Mary, well…"

"So?" Simon said simply.

"What do you mean?" Matt demanded.

"I mean that the Mary thing is really bad," Simon explained. "But *what* are you going to do about it, exactly?"

"I'm going to be a big brother again," Matt replied. "I'm going to try to help Mom and Dad out by keeping an eye on things."

"Things?" Ruthie asked. "What things?"

"Just…*things!*" Matt said, throwing up his hands.

"Weren't you living here with your eye on things when Mary snuck out and went to a frat party?" Simon said. "And weren't you around when Mary skipped school, shoved a guy's head in a toilet, and wrecked the car?"

Simon paused to let Matt catch up. His older brother could be pretty dense at times.

"No offense, but we were doing okay, or at least as bad, without *you* here."

Matt was stung by Simon's words, mostly because they were true.

"If I were here, I might have seen this Mary thing coming," Matt said half-heartedly.

"Well," Ruthie shrugged. "That's not *always* true."

Matt messed his sister's hair. "How would you know?"

"We've been told that it's not always possible to see these things ahead of time," Simon explained, remembering the words of Father Hartman and Rabbi Cohen.

"All that means is that sometimes it *is*," Matt argued.

This time, it was Matt's words that stung. Simon and Ruthie burped.

"Oh, no," Ruthie gasped.

Simon sighed. "It's guilt gut."

"Dinner is served," Mrs. Camden announced as she pushed through the back door, balancing three pizza boxes. She plopped them down on the kitchen table.

"*Three* pizzas?" Reverend Camden asked.

"Cheese, pepperoni, and pineapple,"

said Mrs. Camden, hanging up her jacket.

Reverend Camden looked at his wife. "Ruthie!" they said together.

While Reverend Camden fished the silverware out of the drawer, Mrs. Camden raced around the kitchen, getting plates and napkins with quick, nervous movements.

"Are you okay?" he asked.

"I stopped by the gym," she said.

"I did the same thing earlier," Reverend Camden confessed. "And from the look on your face, we had the same reaction."

Mrs. Camden slammed the plates down on the table. "I know the criminal justice system's options," she began. "And I know what the school can do.

"But what are *we* supposed to do? Ground her? Take away her phone and television privileges. It just doesn't seem to be enough."

She rubbed her tired eyes. "Of course, if by some miracle she doesn't go to jail and just gets expelled, some of those things might be more relevant, but until then..."

Reverend Camden took her in his arms.

"I know, I know," he whispered.

"Do I smell pizza?"

It was Matt.

"Hi, stranger," Mrs. Camden said, hiding her tears.

"It's funny you should use that particular word, because Matt has decided to move back home," Reverend Camden announced.

Matt smiled and nodded. Then he moved to the pizza and grabbed a thick, runny slice. He eagerly took his first bite on the way to the living room.

When Matt was gone, Mrs. Camden turned to her husband.

"Why is he moving back?" she demanded.

"To help out."

"I love Matt, and this will always be his home," Mrs. Camden said with a weary sigh. "But—"

"I feel the same way," her husband assured her. "Do you want me to throw him out?"

"No!" Mrs. Camden cried, horrified. "But I do want you to find out what else is going on with him. This isn't natural."

"I have some other news," Reverend Camden announced ominously.

"We won the lottery."

"I love your sense of humor," he

replied. "But we didn't win the lottery. Mary lost her scholarship."

Mrs. Camden walked to her husband and put her hand on his arm.

"I know this is bad," she said, her voice breaking. "Very, very bad. But none of this matters very much compared to the possibility that Mary could go to jail.

"Of course," she added hopefully, "if Mary *does* go to jail, she can probably pursue a nice vocational skill."

As hard as she fought it, the tears returned. "I thought I was an okay parent. I thought I knew my kid. But I didn't."

The phone rang.

"I'm afraid to answer it," Mrs. Camden said. "Do we know where all of our kids are?"

Reverend Camden thought about it. "Approximately," he said. Then he lifted the receiver.

It was Bill Mays. Reverend Camden listened to the lawyer for a long time. Then he smiled. "You're kidding!" he cried.

Mrs. Camden watched her husband hopefully.

"Okay," he said into the phone. "I'll tell her. And thank you, Bill. Thanks a lot."

Mrs. Camden was on her husband the moment he hung up.

"Bill called in a lot of favors and walked Mary's application through the red tape," he told her. "Now the head of the probation department is willing to meet with us tomorrow."

"Tomorrow!" Mrs. Camden cried, her eyes wide. "You're kidding?"

"Nope. Tomorrow afternoon, right after church."

Mrs. Camden let out a long breath. "So, Mary has a chance at the Diversion Program?"

"Just one chance," he replied. "A small one."

Mrs. Camden met her husband's gaze. "I'll take it."

FIFTEEN

Matt closed the textbook and stretched. He'd been working so long he hadn't noticed how stiff his muscles were getting. Simon's desk was too small for him, but Matt managed to get his work done anyway.

Compared to his apartment—*former apartment*, Matt reminded himself—the Camden house had been pretty quiet since everyone returned from church.

Too quiet, Matt decided.

He headed downstairs.

Matt had to be at work in three hours. Which meant he still had plenty of time to grab lunch and join Mom and Dad and Mary at the meeting with the probation officer.

In the refrigerator, Matt found two pieces of pizza left over from the night before. Unfortunately, they both had pineapple on them.

He grabbed the bologna, a jar of mayonnaise, the Swiss cheese, and a carton of milk. After raiding the bread basket, Matt assembled his lunch.

He stood back and admired his handiwork before taking a huge bite.

While he chewed, Matt spotted a laundry basket brimming with clean and folded clothes. On top of the pile was his now-spotless hospital uniform.

"Thank you, Mom!" he shouted to the empty room.

"You can thank *me*," Lucy announced, walking through the doorway. She was carrying another laundry basket full of clothes, but these were dirty.

She placed the basket on the floor and took a sip of Matt's milk. "I did a couple of color loads yesterday, and Mary went to the grocery store last week, so I guess you should thank her, too."

"Your point?"

Lucy leaned against the table and contemplated the glass in her hand. "Oh, I don't *have* one," she answered with mock innocence. "But you'll be glad to know I've moved on to the whites now."

"Well, thanks. I guess."

Uncomfortable with the direction the conversation was taking, Matt decided to change it. He looked around.

"So, where is everybody?"

"Simon and Ruthie went over to the park as soon as we got home from church," Lucy said. "They said they were too nervous about Mary's big interview to sit around the house."

"Mom and Dad and Mary didn't leave yet, did they?" Matt said, suddenly alarmed.

"They're gone," Lucy said. "Long gone."

"But I was going to go with them," Matt moaned. "To kind of help out."

Lucy studied him curiously. "Uh, they seemed to have everything under control when they left."

She put the now-empty glass on the kitchen table and picked up the laundry basket again.

"Can I help?" Matt offered.

"Help?" she called over her shoulder. "Help with *what?*"

"With nothing," Matt muttered when Lucy was gone.

After lunch, maybe I'll go over and visit Shana, he decided. *She'll be glad to see me—that is, if she's not still mad at me.*

Mary had the feeling that she was locked in a revolving nightmare that had no beginning, and would never, ever end.

She was walking down a long corridor that looked like the halls of a prison. The walls were painted a dull, dirty gray. The furniture—what little there was—consisted mostly of battered metal chairs with stained plastic cushions.

On the wall was a black-framed portrait of the president. The glass covering the picture was stained and dirty, too.

Mary walked along the dull green linoleum. Each step echoed dully off the concrete walls.

She remembered a poem she read in literature class. A poem about Hell called Dante's *Inferno*. In the poem, Hell had many circles, where sinners were punished for all eternity, depending on their crimes.

What circle of Hell am I in now? she wondered.

She walked with both her parents. But despite their presence, Mary had never felt so alone.

She shivered.

Her father seemed to sense her fear, and he rested his hand on her arm. "You'll be okay," he whispered.

Then he paused and said, "This is the place."

Mary read the name on the door.

JENNIFER WILLIAMS, PROBATION OFFICER.

Reverend Camden pushed on the door. Inside was a small, empty waiting room.

"Come in," an unseen, no-nonsense voice called from an adjoining office. "I'll be with you in a minute."

As they sat down, the metal furniture creaked.

The office was sparse. The concrete walls were painted the same shade of depressing gray as the halls, and the floor was the same shade of sickly green.

Mary nervously played with her fingers.

A hard-faced, dark-haired woman entered. She was wearing a severe suit that looked, to Mary, almost like a uniform.

A prison guard's uniform, she couldn't help imagining.

The woman walked right over to Mary, who shifted uncomfortably under the woman's gaze. Mary felt like a virus under a microscope. Steeling her courage, Mary rose slowly to her feet and faced the woman.

"I'm assuming you're Mary."

Mary nodded. "And these are my parents," she added.

The woman looked at Reverend Camden, then at his wife. "Nice to meet you," she said, but her tone was far from warm. "I'm Ms. Williams."

Her sharp eyes focused on Mary again. "You," she said. "You're with me."

Mrs. Camden and her husband began to rise, but Ms. Williams stopped them.

"I know she's your baby and probably always will be a baby—to *you*," Ms. Williams said bluntly. "But she isn't a baby to *me*."

The woman tapped the file folder in her hand. "Mary is seventeen and she's not in your house now, Reverend and Mrs. Camden—she's in mine."

Mary swallowed uneasily when she saw the look on her parents' faces. They were terrified, she realized, for *her*.

Mary tensed. A cold sweat broke over her brow. *I've got to get through this*, she told herself. *For my family's sake*.

Ms. Williams turned and walked into

the adjoining office. She paused in the doorway, waiting for Mary to follow.

I did this, thought Mary. *And now I've got to find a way to undo it.* With her fists clenched and her back straight, she walked slowly into the inner office.

Ms. Williams slammed the door behind her.

Shana had been cleaning her apartment for the last hour when she heard the knock on her door. Though she wasn't expecting visitors, Shana had a pretty good idea of who was calling.

She yanked the bandanna out of her hair, tossed the dust mop in the corner, and pulled open the door.

"Hello, Matt," she said.

Matt shifted on his feet. "I'm just here to say that it doesn't matter who was right or wrong in our argument—"

"We had an argument?" Shana said.

"Okay," Matt said. "Call it a discussion. A discussion you walked out on."

Shana nodded.

"Anyway," Matt continued, "it doesn't matter who was right or wrong because the bottom line is, my family doesn't need me anymore. For anything."

"What are you talking about?"

Matt led Shana to the couch. "I'm like the appendix of family members. Just take me out and not only does everything function without me, it's like I was never there at all! I now know that there is no role of any kind for me in my own family. Not anymore."

"That's not true and you know it," Shana insisted. "You'll always have a role in your family, but roles change. You'll just have to figure out what your new role is going to be."

"You were also right about the rest of what you said, too," Matt added. "I was so busy trying to be a man by taking care of my family, that I was trying to duck out on the part of being a man where you take care of, and claim responsibility for, *yourself*."

"That's easier said than done," Shana said. "Especially when your mom's a great cook."

"Thanks," Matt said, taking her hand. "And I'm sorry for getting angry."

Then he kissed her.

"Umm," Matt sighed. "You smell great. Is that perfume?"

"Lysol detergent," Shana chuckled.

"It's amazing how wonderful household cleansing items can smell," Matt quipped.

"You could help me clean," she suggested.

"Can't. Sorry," Matt said. "I've gotta go. I'm off to John's, to apologize for being such a loser and to kick his new roommate out."

Shana made a fist and punched him gently on the shoulder. "That's the spirit!"

Sitting in Ms. Williams's office, Mary tried not to squirm, but it was hard. The silence was starting to get to her.

Ms. Williams had done nothing but leaf through her file since the door closed and she sat down behind the desk.

Mary cleared her throat. Loudly.

Ms. Williams looked up. Her eyes seemed to see right into Mary's being. She felt herself shrinking under the woman's gaze.

"Someone must really like you," Ms. Williams said, her tone as sharp as her eyes. "You cannot begin to imagine the kinds of favors it took to get me in here on a Sunday."

Ms. Williams closed Mary's file. "What

happened to your grades?" she asked. "Drugs?"

"No!" Mary said emphatically. "Of course not."

"Booze, then? Or a boyfriend you can't get enough of?"

"No," Mary insisted. "None of that."

"It sure was something, because these grades really took a tumble."

Mary shifted in her chair.

"Did you see something at the movies that you had to copy? Or did Marilyn Manson hypnotize you with his songs?"

Mary refused to reply.

"It's your parents," the woman said finally. "They just don't love you enough, right?"

"No," Mary cried.

"I heard about the team lockout and everything. So, I'm guessing the coach and the school did you wrong and so you had to get back at them."

Ms. Williams was getting dangerously close to the truth. But Mary found herself saying, "No…no…" And she realized she actually meant it.

Mary knew why she and her teammates had done it—of course it was because they'd been angry. But the way Ms.

Williams was phrasing the question—it seemed like a childish excuse. Something a little girl would do—trying to get back at someone for not getting her way.

Whether it was the intense scrutiny of this woman or her own conscience, Mary felt a sobering sense of maturity overtake her. And shame.

She felt her hands begin to shake so she clasped them tightly together and took a deep breath.

"Come on, Mary," Ms. Williams goaded. "There must be some reason you did this that has nothing to do with it being your fault."

Mary shook her head, battling back tears.

Ms. Williams backed off. When she spoke again, her tone was civil, but not gentle.

"Why should I consider you for the Diversion Program? Why should the system cut you any kind of break?"

"I...I'm not sure," Mary said. "I've made mistakes, but for the most part, I've always been a pretty good kid."

"Pretty good kids don't trash other people's property," the woman scoffed. "Your answer's not good enough. What else have you got?"

The probation officer opened the folder again. Mary could almost hear those prison bars closing behind her...

SIXTEEN

In another part of town, a bald man in orange robes smiled at a little boy's question. Behind him, a Buddhist temple gleamed under the day's bright sun. He looked down at the boy and his sister and his benevolent smile grew.

"You're not Buddhists, are you?" he asked them.

"No," Ruthie Camden said, pointing at the temple. "But I sure like what you've done with the place."

The priest thought about Simon's question. "Okay," he said. "If you jump into a lake to save a drowning man, but don't get to him in time, it's not your fault if the man is lost."

"Yeah," Simon nodded. "That's true I guess."

"That's what happened with your sister," the priest explained. "You meant to do the right thing, but you can't control everything that happens. Sometimes, you can't even see what *might* happen.

"If you mean to do the right thing," the priest continued, "and try very hard to do the right thing, your lights won't get any dimmer. In short, you did your best, so there is no reason for you to have guilt gut."

"And that's *it?*" Simon said.

"Well," the priest chuckled. "That is really only a tiny part of Buddhism, but maybe you should meditate on what you can do to avoid making the same mistakes again. It will help you become a better person, not only in this life, but in the next one."

Ruthie looked up. "You mean we get more than one chance at this?"

"We believe that the soul moves on from lifetime to lifetime, always searching for enlightenment."

"Wow!" Ruthie exclaimed. "That's good to know."

"Thank you very much," Simon said. "For everything."

"There is one more thing," the man said. "We Buddhists believe that we're all connected, and that we are most connected to our families. So you need to talk to your parents about this. You will feel better when you do."

"I knew he was going to say that," Simon sighed.

"Don't worry about it," Ruthie insisted. "If we don't get it right in this life, then we'll just get it right in the next one."

As they started off for home, Simon turned his eyes toward Heaven. "Thank you," he said.

He hoped that God was listening.

Across town, Reverend Camden and his wife had been nervously waiting for a door to open.

When it did, they nervously watched their daughter walk through it with downcast eyes. Behind her walked the woman who was about to pronounce her fate.

"I don't know what kind of senior year you *thought* you were going to have," Ms. Williams said flatly to Mary. "But now your senior year belongs to me. I'll let you know just how many of the years after it are mine, too."

Mary nodded. Ms. Williams turned. Then the office door slammed, and Mary was alone with her parents. She swallowed uneasily and faced them.

"Ms. Williams has to process my paperwork and assign me to counselors and classes and stuff," Mary said. "But I'm in the program."

Reverend Camden and his wife exhaled for the first time in what felt like days. Then he turned his eyes upward. "Thank you," he whispered.

He knew God was listening.

"Hey, man!" John Hamilton cried. "*Test* the mattress, don't break the bed."

But Mark Carlington ignored him and continued to bounce up and down on the mattress.

There was a knock at the apartment door.

To John's surprise, Matt was there, clutching a brown paper bag.

"Sorry about just dropping in like this."

"It's okay," John replied. "This is still your place. At least until the end of the month."

"Listen," Matt began. "I'm really sorry about everything and, if it's okay with you, I'd like to go on living here."

John smiled instantly. "Okay, Carlington," he said, gleefully hustling the man out the door. "This just isn't going to work out."

"But—"

"Welcome home," John said to Matt after he slammed the door in Mark Carlington's face.

"I got us a little something to celebrate." Matt pulled a bottle of detergent out of the bag and waved it in John's face.

"Great!" John said. "And I've got something to show you." He swung the refrigerator door open. Inside was a loaf of bread, a package of bologna, another package of cheese, a jar of peanut butter and another jar of jelly.

"I'm sorry for being such a jerk," Matt said. "You're one of my best friends and a really great guy. You deserved more respect and consideration than I gave you."

"It's cool," John said. "I thought about moving back home a million times, so I can't blame you for doing the same thing."

It was late afternoon before the Camdens

returned home with Mary, who immediately holed herself up in her room, as she'd done for the last two days.

An hour later, Reverend and Mrs. Camden were sitting on the couch when Simon and Ruthie appeared in the foyer. Mrs. Camden looked up from her knitting. "Mary got into the program," she announced.

Simon burped. Ruthie burped a moment later. "Excuse me," she said.

"What's wrong?" Mrs. Camden asked.

"None of this would ever have happened if it weren't for me," Simon said miserably.

"Us!" Ruthie added. "We're in this one together."

"How could this be *your* fault?" Reverend Camden asked, baffled.

"We eavesdropped on Mary." Simon was speaking so quickly that his words were running together. "We heard her say something was pretty extreme, and we didn't know what it meant, but we knew it meant something probably bad, and we were going to tell you, but we forgot because we went to guys' night at Matt's."

Simon's shoulders sunk. "So, the whole thing is really my fault," he concluded.

"And we really should have told you sooner," Ruthie added. "But you were already busy with Mary, and we both had a finger problem, and we didn't want you to get mad."

"And, of course, there's my bad heart to consider," Reverend Camden added.

"I'm really sorry, Dad," Simon said.

"Me, too," Ruthie nodded. "And we both have guilt gut."

"So why did you confess now?" Reverend Camden asked.

"We talked to a bunch of God's people and tried to do what they said," Simon explained. "So God would know we were sorry and maybe make us feel better—you know. In the gut?"

"And not make us go to," Ruthie paused. "Well, you know where. A place that's like a campfire where you have fun making s'mores, but it's not fun because *you're* the s'mores."

"I know you've been doing some questioning," Reverend Camden said. "The people you talked to are friends of mine, and they called to let me know you were out repenting."

"Only nothing they said worked,"

Simon complained. "We still have guilt gut."

"It's one thing to *say* the right words," Reverend Camden explained patiently. "But you will both learn as you get older that it's another thing to *live* them. And that's tough to do in a couple of days. Living them is something you do over the course of your whole life."

Just then, the front door opened and Matt rushed in. "What happened? What'd I miss?"

"Mary got in the program," Mrs. Camden said.

Matt whistled and sat down. "That's great."

"And you two didn't do anything wrong," Reverend Camden told Simon and Ruthie.

"Except for the lie you told about your destination," Mrs. Camden added. "What if something had happened to you on the way back from the synagogue or the temple? No one would have known where to look for you because you lied about going to the park."

"It was my idea," Simon said. "Ruthie only did it because I did it."

"Oh, no you don't," Ruthie protested. "I made my own choices and helped with the lying, all by myself, and I'm sorry, too."

"It's okay," Mrs. Camden said. "I forgive you. The road to salvation is a bumpy one. How's your guilt gut feeling?"

"It started feeling better"—Simon paused, then sighed with the realization— "right after I talked to you."

"And for the record," Reverend Camden added, "Mary's situation was never your fault, okay?"

"Dad's right," Matt chimed in. "It wasn't your fault because it was mine."

Everyone stared at him.

"I knew Mary was mad," Matt explained. "And if I hadn't been so into my own life, my classes, and my apartment, I would've seen it coming."

"Sorry," Reverend Camden said. "It wasn't your fault, either, son. Because it was really *my* fault."

SEVENTEEN

Lucy, who was upstairs watching the twins, heard loud voices arguing in the living room.

She was dying to find out what was going on now. Lucy double-checked David and Samuel, who were sound asleep. She located the baby monitor, activated it, and rushed down to see what all the noise was about.

She collided with Mary at the bottom of the stairs. Mary had been lurking in the foyer, spying on the rest of the family.

"What are you do—?"

Mary grabbed her arm and pulled Lucy into the living room. "C'mon!"

When they reached the center of the

family circle, Mary cried: "Okay, everyone, just stop!"

She waved a finger under her father's nose. "This wasn't your fault!" she announced.

Then Mary whirled and faced Simon. "And it wasn't your fault, either. It wasn't your fault, or yours, or yours!" she cried to every member of the Camden family.

Ruthie took a surprised step backward. "Whoa!"

"And I'm sorry!" Mary cried. "I'm sorry I did it. I'm sorry for the way I've been acting, and I'm sorry for everything everyone has had to go through because of me.

"And it kills me to know that the word 'sorry' doesn't make any difference. It doesn't undo what I did, and it doesn't make my family like me again."

Mary dropped into an empty chair.

"Hang on," Reverend Camden said. "We—"

"I *know* you *love* me," Mary said. "But how could you *like* me? I don't even like myself. And I don't know how to make things better."

"Be very sorry," Simon told her. "Then do an act of contrition, like meditate to get your light brilliant again, and, finally, learn from your mistakes."

"But most important," Ruthie added, "just be normal."

Mary stared at them with perplexed patience, then shrugged. "Sure. Okay."

"Do you feel better?" Ruthie asked.

"Not really."

Simon sighed. "That's how it works, sometimes."

"I'm sorry for everything," Mary continued. "Including putting more stress on your heart, Dad. I know losing my scholarship made it worse."

"Yeah," said Simon. "I'm really sorry, too. About the finger and all."

"And I'm sorry about the finger thing," Ruthie chimed in. "And the guy thing, and—"

"Oh, SAVE IT!" Reverend Camden exploded, leaping to his feet. "Just save it, all of you!"

Everyone jumped as his voice boomed off the walls, just like it did in church. Only this time he didn't need amplifiers!

Mrs. Camden was chuckling as Reverend Camden put his fingers to the carotid artery in his neck, then to the pulse at his wrist.

"See!" he said, throwing up his hands.

"Nothing. My voice is strong—as you have all heard. My pulse is steady, and I feel *great!*"

"That's good, Dad, but—"

"You can all stop worrying about me and live your lives!" Reverend Camden continued. "But if you *can't* stop worrying, if you feel that you have to keep secrets from me and end-run me with your problems, that's fine, too. My stride is long, my hips are wide. God designed me for the *long* race."

He put his hands on his hips and stared his family down.

"Just remember," Reverend Camden warned them. "When you leave this room, this house, and even this zip code, and you're running around all unfettered and free, that you are all my blood. And blood follows blood."

"Yuck," Ruthie moaned.

"So," he continued, his voice calmer, but no less forceful. "When you finally get to that place behind my back where you're so *desperate* to get, don't be surprised to find me already there. Because I've been a guy who's had a heart attack for a few months, but I've been your father for many, many years and *I know you people.*

"Oh, yes," Reverend Camden concluded. "I *know* you. And I know your *ways*. So listen up, and make room for Daddy, 'cause Daddy's *home!*"

Folding his arms over his chest, he finally sat back down on the couch, an expression of smug satisfaction on his face. Then he turned to his wife.

"I'm back, baby," he said.

"Oh, baby," she said happily. "Don't I *know* it."

"Okay," Lucy said as she followed Mary into the foyer. "There is only one explanation. Our dad has completely lost it."

Mary shook her head sadly. "Wow."

Matt, Simon, and Ruthie brought up the rear. All of them met on the stairs.

"Simon," Matt said, rubbing his brother's head. "You were quite a man in there. Taking responsibility for everything and for trying to protect Ruthie."

Simon shrugged as if it were nothing. "I just did what I figured Dad would do," he said.

Ruthie nodded. "Me, too."

He grinned at them both. "It might be the light," Matt said, tugging on Simon's sweatshirt. "But is that a chest hair I see?"

"Probably," Simon replied. To his surprise, Ruthie was nodding in agreement. Simon went up the stairs.

When he was gone, Ruthie put her hand to Matt's ear. "It was probably just sweatshirt fuzz, but why kill his dream?"

Matt chuckled. "You're a good man, Ruthie."

"Thanks," she cried. "It's really hard with you being gone, but I do what I can."

Ruthie ran up the stairs after Simon.

"Hey, Ruthie!" Matt called from the bottom of the steps. "Thanks for missing me."

Ruthie shrugged. "I can't help it."

Matt smiled. Ruthie's words seemed to travel beyond his ears and all the way down to his heart.

Reverend Camden and his wife were getting ready for bed when there was a knock on the bedroom door.

Matt peeked his head through a crack. "I just wanted to say thanks," he began. "Thanks for dinner, the use of the washing machine, and everything else."

"You're always welcome, honey," Mrs. Camden replied.

"But now," Matt continued, "I think I'm

going to head home—to my apartment."

Matt hugged his mother, then shot his father a big thumbs-up. "Keep up the good work, Dad," he said before departing.

"What happened to his moving back home?" Mrs. Camden wondered aloud.

"I guess my speech probably reassured him," Reverend Camden replied smugly.

"It *was* really something," Mrs. Camden said. "For *all* of us."

Mrs. Camden looked up. "Was that Mary?"

"Hey, you," Reverend Camden called. Mary peeked through the door. She was scratching her head and yawning.

"What are you doing up so late?" he asked.

"I can't turn off my head and go to sleep. I'm worried about coming up with the money to pay the fines. And then there's college. Though if I get expelled, I guess I could take the GED and get a full-time job."

As Mary spoke, she got more and more agitated.

"Calm down," her father said.

"I tried," Mary replied. "But unlike Lucy—who is, no doubt, sleeping like a baby—I'm worried about what's going to happen in student court tomorrow. What if I get expelled?"

"Whatever happens, we'll deal with it," Reverend Camden assured her.

"I know I blew it," Mary said. "But up until now, I've been a pretty good kid, and now, it's gone...all gone. Who knew that one mistake could completely ruin your life?"

"Your Dad and I," said Mrs. Camden. "When you're an adult, you discover that one mistake *can* ruin your life."

Then she smiled. "But I want you to understand that your life isn't ruined, Mary.

"It's going to be different. Radically different. But only you can decide it it's going to be a good different or a bad different."

"Well," Mary corrected her. "Me and Ms. Williams—"

Mrs. Camden smiled.

"—And Ms. Russell and Lucy."

Reverend Camden kissed his daughter's forehead. "We'll deal with it. I promise."

The next day, Mary was walking down a long corridor again. Her parents stood on either side of her once more, but this time the halls weren't strange or empty. These halls were familiar. And they were very crowded.

Mary could feel everyone watching her as she moved toward the high school auditorium. As she passed groups of students, some pointed at her and whispered to one another.

Then she saw Karen and Corey. Both of them looked glum. Their parents were there, too. Maggie arrived, too, her mother in tow. The defiance had gone out of all her friends' eyes. Like Mary's, it had been replaced with fear, worry, and regret.

Inside the auditorium, the seats were filled. Mary could see that TV reporter Carrie Chadwick's pressure had worked on the school board. The woman received permission to cover the student trial for Channel Eight news.

Mary sighed. Now her public humiliation was complete.

The court was set up as before. Lucy sat at the table with the other members of student court. In the first row, Rod and Shelby gave Lucy a thumbs-up. They were there for moral support.

Ms. Russell presided over the court. She sat at the center of the table, a large stack of folders before her. She scanned the room, then raised the gavel and banged it on the table.

"This afternoon's court session will be devoted to dealing with the acts committed against the school by some members of the girls' basketball team," the principal began.

"While I will take everything that's said into consideration, the final ruling will be mine, and mine alone. That decision will be made on Wednesday. The students and their families will be notified first, then my ruling will be posted on the bulletin board."

Principal Russell paused.

"According to the police report, those present were caught in the act of vandalizing the gym. According to the insurance report, total damage to the gym and surrounding structure was assessed at four thousand, three hundred and fifty dollars."

The principal shot a hard look at the girls lined up before her. *"Thank you* for sparing the floors."

That comment brought an explosion of voices. Ms. Russell banged the gavel and called for order.

"Are any of these accounts in dispute?" Ms. Russell asked.

The girls exchanged looks. Then,

together, they turned to Mary, their team captain. Maggie shook her head. So did Karen and Elaine. Corey thought about it for a minute, then shook her head, too.

Mary smiled with new pride at her teammates, then faced the principal.

"No, Ms. Russell," Mary said in a clear voice. "They are not in dispute."

"Okay," Ms. Russell said. "Is there anything else then?"

The room was quiet for what seemed like an eternity. Then Lucy slowly lifted her hand. Ms. Russell appeared surprised.

"I have something to say," Lucy told the principal softly.

"Very well," said Ms. Russell. "Lucy Camden," she announced to the crowded room.

Lucy rose to her feet, locked eyes with her sister a moment, then began to speak to the room. "There are a couple of things I'd like Ms. Russell to consider. I'm in the unique position of seeing a lot of the sides of this case. My sister is the captain of the Lady Wildcats, and even though we fight and argue, and I've never told her this, I've always admired her."

Mary's eyebrows rose as if she could not believe her ears.

"She's also one of the people who trashed the school gym." Lucy paused and looked around the room. The faces were grim, some even hostile, but all of them were listening intently.

"I saw that gym afterward," said Lucy. "And I also saw my family afterward. The thing is, my sister's mistake not only screwed up *her* life, but my whole family's."

Lucy paused again. This time her eyes returned to Mary.

"She learned, and, because of her, my brothers and sister and I learned that one single mistake can ruin your life. And when I thought about it, it made sense."

Lucy turned to face Ms. Russell.

"What I didn't expect, though, was how much someone else's mistake could ruin other people's lives, too. You trash a school gym for whatever reason, and everyone at this school, including your innocent teammates, loses a team, a gym, and the feeling that they are safe at school."

Lucy turned to the audience again.

"That made me mad," she said, her eyes hard. "Mad enough to want to do something. And it would be easy to make these guys write a check and then kick them out!"

Lucy stared at the Lady Wildcats.

"But this is *your* school, too," she said softly, to every one of them. "And I want you to make up for what you did to *all* of us—if only by showing up every day in the hall as examples of the best and worst we can be, and by reminding us all of how close we are, on any given day, to both."

Lucy's eyes caught her father's.

"Gandhi said we're supposed to be the change we want to see in the world," she said, remembering her father's recent words to her. "So, maybe part of the way you can make things up to us is by showing the rest of us how....It's probably an unbelievably hard thing to do," Lucy added, her voice stern, "but if anyone can do it, my *sister* can."

Mary looked at Lucy, and saw her sister's love shining out of her like a brilliant beacon.

At that moment, Mary knew that no matter what happened—no matter what Principal Russell or Ms. Williams, or anyone else decided to do to her—she would always have a family, and a sister, who loved her.

In the end, that was all that really mattered.

EIGHTEEN

When student court was finally adjourned, Mary knew what she had to do.

She led the Lady Wildcats out of the student courtroom and toward the wrecked gymnasium.

In the doorway to the gym, Mary paused. With new eyes, she looked at the damage she'd done to the gym, the school, her family, and herself.

She hoped Principal Russell would take Lucy's advice and decide not to expel her and her teammates. But Lucy wasn't the only person who could convince Ms. Russell to give the Lady Wildcats another chance.

As team captain, Mary faced her friends. Karen, Maggie, and the others nodded silently. She led them into the shattered gym.

An example. To show us all the best and worst that we can be.

With Lucy's words fresh in her mind, Mary decided that from now on, she would try to be an example of the *best* a person could be.

The janitor looked up in surprise as Mary took the broom from his hand and began to sweep.

Around her, the Lady Wildcats followed her example, picking up the garbage strewn across the floor.

It was a clear act of contrition.

MARY'S STORY

Big sis Mary seems to have it all together:
She's practical, super-smart, beautiful, viva-
cious, and a rising star on her school's basketball team. But beneath her perfect
exterior, sixteen-year-old Mary is struggling
to figure out boys, friends, parents, and life
in general—not to mention her younger
sister Lucy!

MATT'S STORY

As the oldest kid in the Camden clan and a college freshman, handsome eighteen-year-old Matt often bears the burden of playing referee between his siblings and his parents. Sometimes it's tough to balance family loyalty against a fierce desire for independence, but Matt has earned his reputation as the "responsible one"—*most* of the time.

RIVALS

For better or for worse, Mary and Lucy
Camden have one thing in common:
they're the oldest sisters in a *huge*, busy
family! But sometimes the two of them
hardly seem related: strong, independent
Mary hangs out on the basketball court,
while sensitive, impulsive Lucy loves the
mall. And when there's a cute guy involved,
it's all-out war!

Turn up the heat and the

volume!

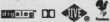